"Why are you trying to pick a fight?"
Jordan asked.

Sarajane's chin went up. "I'm not picking a fight. I'm trying to make you better."

There was something about the way she looked when she became so incensed that aroused him. And goaded him on. "You'd be the first to complain about me."

"I'm not one of the bimbos you squire," she informed him indignantly. "I'm a real person."

Something rippled through him as she drew in another breath. "You are at that."

He had no idea how it happened. How the heated words that were being exchanged like gunfire led him to take the next step. This was an argument about nothing. Nothing except the elephant in the living room: the very strong attraction he felt toward her.

Because one minute, he was engaged in a duel of words. The next, there were no words.

The kiss took center stage.

Dearest Reader,

So glad you could take this opportunity to join me on the next installment of the latest Logan series. Some of you might remember meeting Jordan Hall when I wrote about his sister Jenny in the last series. Jordan was the good guy who put up the money in a bachelor auction so that, unbeknownst to his sister, she would get a date with the man of her dreams—his best friend, Eric. Well, any guy that thoughtful (where *do* you get brothers like that?) deserves a story—and a lady—of his own.

In this tale, he gets both. We watch an already good guy find the true meaning in life, not rich clients he can handily get off the hook, but poor, deserving ones who have nowhere to turn.

Because of a difficult pregnancy, Jenny's doctor orders her to bed. Unable to turn her back on her work, she turns to Jordan and pleads with him to fill in until she can find someone permanent. He does and it isn't long before that someone permanent turns out to be him. All because Ms. Sarajane Gerrity opens his eyes—and his heart.

Hope you like this and, as always, I wish you love.

Marie Ferrarella

MARIE FERRARELLA

MR. HALL TAKES A BRIDE

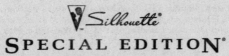

SPECIAL EDITION

Published by Silhouette Books

America's Publisher of Contemporary Romance

Special thanks and acknowledgment are given
to Marie Ferrarella for her contribution to
the LOGAN'S LEGACY REVISITED miniseries.

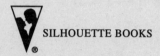

SILHOUETTE BOOKS

®

ISBN-13: 978-0-373-24813-1
ISBN-10: 0-373-24813-X

MR. HALL TAKES A BRIDE

Visit Silhouette Books at www.eHarlequin.com

Printed in U.S.A.

Books by Marie Ferrarella

Silhouette Special Edition

Her Good Fortune #1665
Because a Husband Is Forever #1671
The Measure of a Man #1706
She's Having a Baby #1713
Her Special Charm #1726
Husbands and Other Strangers #1736
The Prodigal M.D. Returns #1775
Mother in Training #1785
*Mr. Hall Takes a Bride #1813

Harlequin Next

Starting from Scratch #17
Finding Home #45
The Second Time Around #73

Silhouette Intimate Moments

In Broad Daylight #1315
Alone in the Dark #1327
Dangerous Disguise #1339
The Heart of a Ruler #1412
The Woman Who Wasn't There #1415
Cavanaugh Witch #1431

Silhouette Romantic Suspense

Her Lawman on Call #1451

*Logan's Legacy Revisited

MARIE FERRARELLA

This *USA TODAY* bestselling and RITA® Award-winning author has written over one hundred and fifty novels for Silhouette, some under the name Marie Nicole. Her romances are beloved by fans worldwide.

To Patience Smith,
my muse, my friend,
with eternal gratitude.

Chapter One

"C'mon, Jordan, please? You owe this to me."

Jordan Hall, high-profile defense attorney and much-sought-after man about town, had been en route to the airport to begin what he felt was a greatly deserved Hawaiian surfing vacation when a frantic call from his younger sister had brought him racing back to Portland and the house that she and her husband, his best friend, Eric Logan, shared with Jenny's six-year-old adopted son, Cole. On the phone, Jenny had made it sound like a matter of life or death.

Now that he had discovered that there was no death, imminent or otherwise, Jordan had pulled himself together, masked his initial concern and looked down at his six-months-pregnant sister, who'd forced herself into a semi-horizontal position on the sofa. Knowing Jenny, it was a compromise. The doctor had probably had a bed in mind when he'd given her strict orders to rest.

Jordan crossed his arms and did his best to look annoyed, but Jenny was just too damn good to be annoyed at. She had a way of bringing out the best in everyone.

But this time, he was doing his utmost to resist.

"How, pray tell, do I 'owe' this to you?" he wanted to know, the "this" in question being temporarily taking her place at Advocate Aid, Inc., and dispensing legal advice with no compensation other than being on the receiving end of a grateful smile. "If we're going to bandy about the subject of 'owing,' it's you who actually 'owe' me, dear sister." He saw her mouth drop open and felt a surge of triumph. Eric, perched on the arm of the sofa next to her, looked mildly amused by the exchange. "If not for me, you might still be buried hip-deep in charity work, never seeing the light of day or having Eric's beatific smile bestowed on you on a daily basis."

"Beatific?" Eric echoed with a wide grin. He fluttered his lashes at him. "Why, Jordan, I never knew you felt that way about me."

Jordan grimaced. "I don't, but for some reason, every card-carrying member of the female sex does. Including my sister," he added needlessly, "your very pregnant wife." Jordan looked pointedly at Jenny, continuing the stroll down memory lane. "If I hadn't 'arranged' to have your friends bid on Eric in that ridiculous bachelors' auction—"

"As I recall, you were part of the auction, too," Eric reminded him.

Jordan shrugged casually. "What can I say? I'm a pushover for charity."

"And wealthy, good-looking women," Jenny was quick to interject. It was a well-known fact that people in the circles Jordan traveled felt that her brother had put the *play* in *playboy*.

Jordan's eyes seemed to twinkle as he obligingly acknowledged, "That, too."

"That foremost," Jenny countered, shifting on the sofa, feeling very much like a prisoner. She was a mover, a shaker. By definition, that sort of personality and calling necessitated mobility. Imitating a still-life painting like this was making her crazy. When she thought about having to do it for the next three months, it was all she could do to keep from screaming. But that would only frighten Cole, so she struggled to contain her edginess.

Jordan looked at her, shaking his head. "Marriage has made you feisty, little sister."

Eric laughed. "Feisti*er*," he corrected his best friend. "Marriage has made her feisti*er*. This woman was never a cupcake."

"Which is why I'm not going to give up." Jenny

congratulated herself on bringing the conversation back to its rightful place, centered on what she both wanted and needed her older brother to do. She'd come to her conclusion after a night of soul-searching. Also a night of calling everyone else she could think of to ask. Giving them first crack at filling in the very vital space. She'd gotten several tentative promises of "next month," but no one was available immediately.

Jordan was her last hope.

"It's only for three weeks," she pleaded earnestly. "That should give me enough time to arrange for someone else to come in and pick up the slack."

"Three weeks," Jordan repeated. The look he gave his sister was fraught with suspicion. "By some odd coincidence, that's also the exact length of my Hawaiian vacation."

"Exactly." Jenny pounced on the lead-in her brother had handed her. "You were slated to go on vacation anyway. This way, you won't miss any time at Morrison and Treherne."

Jordan sat down on the edge of the coffee table, facing his sister, and took her hand between both of his. "Let me define *vacation*, in case a workaholic like yourself has forgotten the meaning of the word. *Vacation*, as in lying on white sandy beaches with crystal-blue water lapping at your toes, a bikinied goddess lying beside you. *Vacation*, as in taking a long, languid cruise, sitting on the uppermost deck beside a pool, a bikinied goddess in the deck chair beside you. *Vacation,* as in—"

Jenny pulled her hand away, glancing over to the far side of the room where Cole was playing with his action figures, afraid he might have overheard. But the little boy she'd taken into her heart as her own when her best friend had died looked completely preoccupied with the world he was creating. "We get the picture."

"Nowhere in that scenario, you might notice," Jordan went on patiently, "does it call for me to be sitting in a two-by-four termite-riddled box, playing bleeding-heart advocate to thugs and criminals."

Jenny sat up ramrod-straight, taking offense for the people she had come to care about as much as she might have cared for distant relatives who needed her help and her understanding.

"Just because they're poor doesn't mean they're thugs and criminals, Jordy. You know that." She looked at him, wondering if he was being serious or if he was just pulling her leg. She decided it had to be the latter. "I refuse to believe that you're that shallow."

That lopsided smile she knew and loved told her that her heart was right. He was pulling her leg. She'd won. He was just playing it out a little longer.

"I can bring you a note from my doctor," Jordan offered.

Two could play this game, Jenny thought. She threw off the blanket that Eric had tucked around her legs. She glanced toward her husband now. "Okay, he leaves me no choice, I have to go in."

Eric put his hands to her shoulders, holding her in place. "You have to have this baby, nothing else. The doctor said you needed bed rest."

But she shook her head. "Those people are counting on me."

"Your baby's counting on you," Eric countered.

Jordan frowned. Jenny had already told him that Advocate Aid were down one lawyer. And there was what he felt amounted to a tempest in a teapot. Jenny had prevailed upon him to give legal advice to a non-profit fertility organization called the Children's Connection. A birth father, Thad Preston, was trying to get his fifteen minutes of fame by saying that his girlfriend gave up their child for adoption without his consent. He claimed to be suing for custody but what he was suing for was attention. It made for juicy reading when he brought his distorted version of the truth to the Portland Gazette.

Once again, the Children's Connection, just recovering from a series of unfortunate events, was cast in a bad light.

But all that was temporary and would pass in time. He didn't see the need to give up his vacation for either organization. "And if Advocate Aid, Inc., has to close its doors for a couple of weeks or three, would that really be such a big deal? Would it make that much of a difference?"

Jenny stared at him. Was he serious? "You know how important time is in a trial. A person's life can be permanently altered in the space of an hour. In the space of two minutes," she emphasized with feeling, thinking about cases where the death penalty was involved. It was organizations such as her own that saw to it that justice was not only served, but equally distributed, even to those who couldn't afford the price of a lawyer.

"Jenny," Jordan began patiently, "you're talking about penny-ante cases. The ones I take all involve high stakes—"

"Name me higher stakes than people's dreams," she challenged. When he didn't answer immediately, she came in for the kill. "Jordy, you're the smartest man I've ever known—no offense, honey," she added, turning to look at Eric.

Broad shoulders rose and fell nonchalantly, accompanied by an amused expression. "None taken."

"Speaking of whom," Jordan's eyes narrowed as he looked at Eric and nodded toward his brother-in-law. "Why can't your illustrious husband get one of his lawyer buddies to take your place until you find someone else?"

Eric looked at him pointedly. "I am."

"Besides me," Jordan amended.

"Everyone else I know with a law degree is wrapped up in some trial or other," Eric told him.

Jordan frowned at him. "How convenient."

"You're the only one with time to spare, buddy," Eric concluded.

"Please, Jordan?" Jenny made another sincere entreaty. "Maybe you won't wind up on the six o'clock news, but who's to say these cases aren't just as important to the people who are involved? Sure, there are cases involving criminal charges, but there are also cases that involve stopping foreclosures. The cases I see also deal with unfair lawsuits that steal everything from the accused, even when they're innocent. Then there's—"

Jordan rolled his eyes and looked at his best friend. He could literally feel his vacation slipping away from him. "She really isn't going to stop until I say yes, is she?"

Eric's amused expression only deepened. "She's your little sister, Jordy. You should know that about her by now."

Yes, he did. He also knew Jenny was a walking heart with legs. He'd never seen anyone who cared so much about her fellow man—and woman—even if they didn't deserve it.

The last glimmer of his vacation faded off into the sunset. Since he was going first-class and had paid top dollar, he could easily exchange his ticket or get a refund. Nothing was being wasted—except for his time, he thought darkly.

But this meant a lot to Jenny.

Okay, how hard could it be? After all, he'd never

lost a case yet and he was willing to bet every last one of his cases were far more complicated than anything he was going to face at Advocate Aid.

"Okay," he said with resignation. "I'll do it."

"Jordy, you're the best!" Leaning forward on the sofa, Jenny threw her arms around his neck.

"Yes, I am." Extricating himself, he rose to his feet. There were things he had to take care of first if he was going to do this for her. "And you'd better name this baby after me."

Cole picked this time to abandon his fighting figures and join them, throwing his arms around his favorite uncle's waist.

"I've got to go, sport," he told the boy, petting Cole's silky hair.

"Even if it's a girl?" Jenny wanted to know, referring to his request.

Jordan nodded, keeping a straight face. "Even if it's a girl. 'Jordan' works both ways these days, remember?"

Jenny smiled for the first time since her brother had arrived at the house. For the first time since the doctor had knocked the air out of her lungs with his newest edict.

"Just as long as you do, that's all that counts." She beckoned him to lean down and when he complied, she brushed her lips against his cheek. "Thanks, big brother, I owe you one."

He straightened, laughing. "You bet you do."

She knew that tone. Somehow, her big brother meant to collect. Jenny looked at her husband. "I kind of feel as if I've just made a deal with Rumpelstiltskin."

"Jordan's taller," Eric deadpanned.

"Also faster," Jordan interjected, making his way to the front door, Cole shadowing his every move. After Eric, he worshipped Jordan most. Neither man could do any wrong in his young eyes. "At least fast enough to beat you at racquetball last week."

Eric bit back a choice colorful word since Cole was in the room. "That was a fluke."

Jordan looked at him smugly. "Would you care for a rematch?"

"Love one," Eric countered. "Meet you at the court at one on Friday?" They had a standing reservation at the racquetball courts every Friday at lunchtime.

Jordan looked at his sister. "Brace yourself for a shattered husband." He pulled opened the front door. "Okay, I've gotta fly."

"Can I watch?" Cole asked eagerly.

"Maybe next time," Jordan laughed, ruffling his hair. "See you, Jen," he called back into the room. "Remember—" he winked when she looked up at him "—you name the baby after me."

As he closed the door behind Jordan, Eric put his arm around Cole and walked back to where Jenny was lying on the sofa. A bemused expression played across his lips. "Don't you think that was a little over the top, threatening to go in despite the doctor's orders?"

She thought she'd been particularly passionate in her declaration. And she'd known Jordan wouldn't allow her to take the risk, no matter how blasé he attempted to be about the matter.

Jenny smiled, satisfied. "It worked, didn't it?"

Eric sat down on the sofa's arm again and kissed the top of his wife's head. "You know, Jordan and I have been friends just about forever and I never knew he was this malleable."

Cole curled up in the space next to Jenny. She tucked her arm around the boy, so grateful for the way her life had turned out. And Jordan was right, she did owe a great deal of it to him. But that admission was for another time.

"You have to know what buttons to press," she told Eric. "Beneath that devil-may-care, playboy exterior there really is a good guy."

Eric laughed under his breath. In his experience, Jordan could stand his ground with the best of them. This was a side he was unaccustomed to. "Lucky for you."

It wasn't herself she was thinking of. "No, lucky for Advocate Aid."

From what Jenny had told Eric about what went on in the small office, it sounded like five times the work for none of the pay. And there were no law clerks to pick up the slack or do any of the research. Something, he knew, Jordan took completely for granted. "Think he can handle it?"

She smiled fondly, thinking of the dynamo who ran the office and oversaw every detail with a keen, discerning eye. "Sarajane will *make* him handle it."

Eric was acquainted with the office assistant only by reputation, secondhand information he'd gleaned from what his wife had told him in passing. Still, what he knew was impressive. And might have been intimidating to a man of lesser confidence than Jordan. Maybe even intimidating to Jordan.

"I kind of feel sorry for him."

Jenny didn't see it that way. "Jordan survived our mother." Although loving, there was no denying that Elaine Winthrop Hall was a very opinionated woman who saw life only in her own terms. "After that, he can handle anything," she replied with certainty.

At least, Jenny added silently, she sincerely hoped so.

When she woke up Monday morning, Sarajane Gerrity knew it wasn't going to be a good day.

The March sky outside her window was an unusually brilliant shade of blue without a cloud in the sky, but she still sensed that something was off kilter in the universe, or going to go off kilter before the day was over. It was pure instinct, some innate way of being able to tell that all was not right with her world.

Not that, she thought as she slapped down the alarm button and dragged herself out of bed, it ever was a hundred percent right. Not with the poverty and the shattered lives that she witnessed parading through the tiny storefront office of Advocate Aid, Inc., five days a week. But at the end of the day, she liked to think, she made a difference in at least a few lives.

Her title was secretary, but that was an archaic term for what she really was: the person who kept track of everything. The person who, at any given moment, knew where to find Jenny Logan, Harry Reed, Sheldon Myers or any one of the myriad forms that were used in the office on an irregular basis.

In the old days, in one of those old movies she loved so much, Sarajane mused, she might very well have been referred to as a Girl Friday. Except that life had gotten a great deal more hectic since those days and now she could be thought of as a Girl Monday through Friday—and then some. There certainly was enough work to fill eighteen hours of each day.

She didn't mind. At twenty-five, she had the energy for it, had the dedication for it. And it made her feel as if her life actually counted for something. It kept her going.

Sarajane had a need to help others, because doing so was her atonement to the two people who had mattered most to her and who she'd watched slip away, little by little, one to the world of alcohol and self-loathing, the other to the destructive oblivion of drugs.

The first had been her mother, the second, her older brother. When they'd died, leaving her on her own, she'd felt incredibly abandoned. Alone, she was able to understand how her mother had felt. Hopeless. Afraid. But she was determined not to let those feelings overwhelm her. Determined not to be swept away into a world of apathy or drowned by hopelessness. Hers was not to be the battle of the bottle, but it was an uphill fight, one that eventually would lead to her triumphing over her circumstances and making something of herself.

These people who trooped through Advocate Aid, Inc., looking lost and hopeless, reminded her so much of her mother, her brother. If she could somehow be instrumental in helping these strangers, then the pain of not being able to do anything to prevent the deaths of the two people who comprised the only family she'd ever known lessened. At least for a little while.

But today wasn't about anything nearly so personal to her. Today, because of the late-evening phone call she'd taken from Jenny, was about battling an awful sinking feeling in the pit of her stomach. She had too much to do to play den mother, but that was what it was going to amount to. She was going to have to take a newbie by the hand and lead him onto the right path. Since this newbie was Jordan Hall, she anticipated the job of acclimating the man to office procedures as being more difficult than wrestling alligators on a slick Everglades bank.

She'd never met Jordan Hall, but she'd dealt with him on the phone a couple of times when he'd called looking for his sister. And she'd seen a picture of him on the society page once. Dark-brown hair, deep-brown eyes, wicked smile. *Movie-star handsome* would best describe him. Movie-star handsome and born with a silver spoon in his mouth. That definitely did not make him a person who could even remotely relate to the kinds of people who came to Advocate Aid seeking help.

Be fair. Jenny comes from exactly the same background.

Yes, but Jenny, Sarajane thought as she hurried through her shower, praying that the hot water would last long enough for her to finish, was a saint. There was no doubt in her mind that Jenny Logan was in a class all by herself. It was too much to hope for that her brother was cast from the same mold.

Sarajane laughed shortly. If he had been, Jordan Hall would have shown up at the office in person a lot sooner, instead of being some disembodied voice on the phone who called once in a blue moon when he was being consulted.

"Beggars can't be choosers," she told her reflection as she quickly passed a blow dryer over her auburn hair. She longed for straight hair as she watched the shoulder-length mass curl in several directions. With Sheldon gone for the next one to two weeks because of some sort of family emergency and now Jenny down for the count—for at least for three months—that left only Harry Reed and her to hold down the fort. She was good and she was quick, but she was not a lawyer. Being sympathetic to a person's plight only went so far. It didn't begin to untangle whatever legal web they found themselves in.

A legal web such as the one that had brought her mother down, forcing her to sell the small house that was all she had after her husband, a driver for the transit authority, had been killed in a freak bus accident. She'd been forced to sell because the relatives of the people who had died in that accident had sued not only the transit authority, but the family of the man they felt was responsible for the accident.

She was going to be late, Sarajane thought, annoyed at the minutes that had somehow managed to disappear. Grabbing her purse, she hurried out the door, heading to the parking garage where she kept her car. It seemed ironic to her that, after having grown up hating all lawyers, she found herself voluntarily working for them. Someday, when she had the time, she was going to have her head examined.

Someday. But not today.

Chapter Two

You win some, you lose some.

The old adage echoed in Jordan's head as he made his way down the streets of a section of Portland he rarely, if ever, passed through.

The problem was, he didn't like losing. Ever. Granted, it wasn't something he was accustomed to doing, certainly not in the courtroom. And not in the bedroom, either.

But he'd kept his cool and said, "Perhaps another time," when he'd broken the news to Gina over the phone after he'd left Jenny and Eric's house yesterday. Gina Rivers, the model whose face graced a hundred magazine covers and whose body was

considered near-perfect by every breathing male between the ages of ten and a hundred, was the woman
who was to meet him in Hawaii. The woman he had
intended to take his now-aborted vacation with.
When he'd called her about the change in plans, she'd
made a few sympathetic noises about how charitable
he was being to his little sister, then coolly told him
not to be concerned about ruining her plans.

Apparently she'd had someone waiting in the
wings all along. There was a prince from one of those
tiny principalities no one outside of *Jeopardy* paid
much attention to who'd been after her to rendezvous
with him for quite some time now. Since *he* was
available at a moment's notice, she saw no reason not
to have him "fill in" as she'd put it.

Obviously all men were merely interchangeable
bodies to her. Jordan didn't particularly like being
replaced so effortlessly. Granted there was no huge
romance in the offing with this woman, no future,
really, but he had anticipated sharing a good time
with the supermodel for the space of three weeks.

For just a second, as he continued driving, the
shallowness of his social life stared him in the face.
He admitted, in the privacy of his mind, that he was
just the slightest bit weary of beautiful, vapid wom-
en. Yes, a good many of them were experts at setting the sheets on fire, but once they were in a
vertical position, there was not much to go on. Certainly not much in common with him. He found

himself a little envious of Eric. Jenny was pretty and she had a soul, not the easiest combination to come across.

Still, he did enjoy himself, and he had been looking forward to this vacation, to shedding the responsibilities that he took very seriously and to just having a little mindless fun and relaxation for twenty-one days.

"You really do owe me big-time, Jen," he murmured under his breath as he craned his neck to make out the faded addresses that graced the fronts of less than half the stores and buildings he passed.

It was hard to imagine, the way the streets were now, that this area had ever been new. The buildings looked as if they had been standing, enduring the less-than-clement Portland weather, for the last century or so.

Here and there Jordan saw half-hearted attempts at renovations, seemingly doomed before they were begun. Cheap paint was slapped onto surfaces to make them look newer than they were and to hide the multitude of flaws.

Oh well, he wasn't here for the view or a tour, he was here for Jenny.

Jenny, the pure of heart, he thought with a smile.

He supposed his sister was right when she insisted that this was their duty. Growing up, they had both always had so much, had never wanted for anything. The best education, the best of everything, really. It only seemed right to try to pay some of it back.

This, Jordan decided, would fill his pro bono quota for the next year.

Maybe longer, he amended, slowing his car down even more as he realized that he was looking at the storefront office where he'd agreed to spend the next three weeks, shepherding the lost and the confused through the maze known as their legal system.

The sign in the window, which Jenny told him had once displayed the wares of an independent clothing store, brightly proclaimed: Advocate Aid, Inc., in bold black letters on gleaming white poster board. It only made the surrounding area appear that much more dingy and forlorn.

To Jenny's credit—at least, he assumed as much— the display window was dust-free and clean, unlike the displays belonging to the businesses on either side of the legal aid office. To the right, ironically enough, he thought, was a pawn shop. The window was crammed with all sorts of things that had once been precious to someone, and that were now being sold in an effort to keep body and soul together. From the amount of dust that had accumulated, Jordan guessed that the items had last seen anything remotely close to a good cleaning somewhere during the Eisenhower era.

To the left of the office was a smaller store front which displayed an anemic blue light. The fixture was fashioned to proclaim that a seer of the future was domiciled just beyond the threshold. For a nominal fee, the secrets of the future could be shared.

Jordan paused, his sports car idling. He shook his head in disbelief. His sister had graduated near the top of her class. She could have had an office next to his at Morrison and Treherne.

"What the hell are you doing here, Jenny?" he wondered out loud.

And what was he doing here? he wondered silently. For that matter, where the hell was he going to park his car? More to the point, was it going to be there when it came time for him to leave? Cars like his were targets in seedy neighborhoods like this. A good team could strip it in no time flat.

Maybe he should have rented an inexpensive car for the next three weeks. Too late now, he thought with a sigh.

A sign indicating that there was parking behind the row of stores had him circling the block, looking for an opening. He missed it the first time around. When he discovered it on his second pass, he found his driving skills challenged. The alleyway that led to the lot was narrow, even for his sports car. He held his breath the entire time.

When he finally reached the lot, Jordan saw that there were several cars already there. Or maybe they'd just been abandoned, he amended, seeing the condition of the vehicle closest to him. It had at least twenty years on it and the years had not been kind.

Getting out, holding a container of cappuccino in one hand, Jordan engaged the security alarm in his car with his other, wondering if the gesture was a futile one. He had a feeling that anyone here probably knew how to disarm such an alarm in a matter of seconds, silencing it before it had a chance to go off.

Here goes nothing, Jordan thought, walking back out onto the street.

He passed a man rolling back the rusted iron security gates that protected the pawn shop from any break-ins. Short, squat, with arms that looked as if bench-pressing an elephant would have presented no hardship to him, the man wore his hair cropped so close to his head it appeared to be almost shaved.

Pausing as he secured the gates, the pawn-shop owner looked at Jordan and then nodded at the display window. "See anything you like?"

Jordan didn't bother looking, although he did return the man's smile. No sense in antagonizing someone whose biceps rivaled the circumference of truck tires. "Not at the moment."

The pawn-shop owner continued staring at him. "Nice threads," he commented. "I could get you a good price for them."

Probably not anywhere in the neighborhood of what he'd actually paid for the Armani suit, Jordan thought. "Thanks. I'll keep that in mind."

"You work there?" the man asked as Jordan put his hand on the doorknob.

"Temporarily."

The man nodded knowingly. "That's what they all say."

Jordan didn't bother to answer.

The door to Advocate Aid, Inc., was unlocked when he tried it. The second he entered, he knew that he had overdressed. The closet of his penthouse apartment was teeming with expensive suits, suits he regarded as part of his trade because his father had impressed on him at an early age that people judged by appearances and the Halls had always been judged well. Wearing a suit was second nature to him—when he wasn't wearing the latest actress or model or drop-dead gorgeous debutante.

But designer suits were definitely out of place in here, he thought, closing the door behind him.

Walking in, he looked around slowly. His first impression didn't improve. The area seemed almost claustrophobically small. His old bedroom in the family estate was bigger than this place that Jenny said had five people working in it when they were running at full capacity.

He didn't understand how *anyone* could get anything accomplished here. It looked like an illustration for chaos. Every inch of the place was filled with books and papers, scattered and bound. Three of the desks had computers, all of which appeared to be on their way to a museum. The desks beneath them looked battle-worn.

Over in the corner there were ancient bookcases

that appeared to be leaning forward, bowing beneath the weight of legal books and, he could only assume from this distance, dust.

It was enough to send someone of his orderly nature out into the street, gasping for air.

Jordan glanced at his watch. Jenny had told him to get here by nine. It was eight-thirty. He was early because that was his nature. He hated to be kept waiting and felt that keeping anyone else waiting was rude. But early or not, he hadn't expected to be the first one here. He looked around again, but there was no one else in the office. Not unless they were hiding beneath the stacks of paper on the floor.

But the door was unlocked, he recalled.

Maybe they had decided to close down after all and someone had just forgotten to lock the doors. Not that there looked as if there was anything to steal here, he thought, looking around again.

A noise coming from the rear of the room caught his attention. It sounded like a door slamming. Maybe there was more to the office than he'd noticed. He was about to make his way to the back when he found himself almost colliding with a petite—she couldn't have been more than five foot one—young woman with auburn hair and incredibly lively green eyes.

Her arms were full of files which she immediately transferred into his.

The woman didn't bother with an introduction.

"Call Mr. Abernathy about tomorrow's hearing.

You have a ten o'clock appointment with Joan Reynolds. Mr. Wyatt wants to know why no one has returned his calls. He's on line two and he's not getting off until he talks to a lawyer." About to take off again, she skidded to a halt in order to add, "Oh, and the temp called in sick again and Harry is stuck in traffic and says he'll get here when he gets here."

Only quick reflexes had Jordan saving himself from an unscheduled close-to-scalding cappuccino bath. He managed to switch hands just before this Energizer Bunny on steroids with the rapid-fire mouth dumped the files on him.

Still shell-shocked, he stared at her now. "Harry?" he repeated. His voice sounded hoarse to his ears.

The woman was frowning. And her eyes were passing over him as if she was judging him—and finding him wanting. "Harry Reed. The other lawyer who works here."

Finished, she turned on her heel, giving every indication that she was about to disappear into the abyss from whence she had emerged.

"Hold it!" Jordan called after her.

Ordinarily, when he took that tone with the law clerks who were interning at Morrison and Treherne, they froze. If they looked up at him at all, it was with meek expressions on their faces. Whoever this whirling dervish was, she only paused in her flight, glancing at him over her shoulder. There was a look of barely suppressed annoyance on her face.

"Yes?"

"Just who the hell are you?" he demanded sternly. He wasn't accustomed to being ordered around, fluffed off or ignored and she had done all three in the space of less than a minute.

"I'm Sarajane." She said the name as if that was supposed to mean something to him. When he made no response, she added her last name impatiently. "Sarajane Gerrity."

The frown on what seemed like an otherwise pretty face deepened. Exasperated, Sarajane turned completely around and crossed back to him. "You *are* Jenny Logan's brother, aren't you? Jordan Hall?"

That was a new one on him. He couldn't remember himself ever having been referred to that way. If anything, Jenny was regarded as "Jordan Hall's sister." He was the one who had garnered fame and attention in the family, not Jenny. To have it stripped away so cavalierly was a completely new experience for him. Apparently, in this small corner of the universe, his sister had come into her own.

Way to go, Jen.

"Yes, I am," he answered.

Sarajane nodded, as if she approved and he had given the right answer to her question. But the slight frown remained. "She said you'd be coming in today to try to help out."

He noticed that she'd said *try*. As if she didn't expect him to accomplish anything. Obviously the woman didn't get out much. Or maybe she just didn't read the local section of the newspaper. The cases he handled appeared in print with a fair amount of regularity. There was talk of making him a partner at the firm the next time around.

"She didn't tell me about you," Jordan countered. Jenny had called him again late last night, to tell him about the office manager or office secretary. He hadn't paid that much attention really. She might have even said the woman's name, he wasn't sure. Besides, office managers weren't people he ordinarily interacted with unless they forgot to order something he needed.

A buzzer sounded behind him. Jordan turned around just as the front door opened. Out of the corner of his eye, he saw the woman with the disapproving expression suddenly transform, as if a magic wand had been waved over her. The frown vanished, replaced by a warm, welcoming smile. She looked positively sympathetic.

And positively beautiful, he realized.

Devoid of her frown, Sarajane Gerrity's features softened. She looked almost radiant. Despite his best efforts not to, he found that his attention was immediately engaged.

Sarajane sailed by him as if he was nothing more than one of the desks or chairs in the place. Her attention seemed to be completely focused on the couple who had just walked in. He looked at the couple now. They appeared to be in their later fifties, possibly early sixties and life had not been kind to either of them.

He caught himself wondering what had brought them here and what had put that close-to-panic look on the woman's face.

"Please, have a seat," Sarajane was saying. She gestured toward two chairs in front of the desk closest to the front door. The desk had an incredible amount of papers piled on it. As she coaxed the couple to sit, Sarajane scooped away one of the piles of paper, depositing it onto the adjacent desk. "I was just about to make some coffee. Can I get either of you a cup?" Sarajane asked.

"No, no coffee." The woman had an accent he couldn't readily place. He watched her open her purse and take out a much-creased packet of papers. "Just help," the woman entreated simply. "We got this in the mail—" she began, holding up the papers.

But Sarajane stayed the woman's hand before she could launch into her tale. She nodded her head toward Jordan. "Mr. Hall over there will be right with you." Retracing her steps back to him, Sarajane took possession of the files again, digging them out of his arms. "These will be waiting for you on the table," she promised. She placed them next to the pile she'd just shifted from the first desk.

It was clear that the walk-ins took precedence over all the other instructions she'd fired at him.

"What about Mr. Wyatt?" he wanted to know. The light on the phone on what she indicated was his desk was blinking almost hypnotically.

Even as he posed the question, another line lit up and began to ring. Followed immediately by another. He had the feeling that this was business as usual in this place.

He looked at Sarajane expectantly and barely heard the sigh that escaped her lips. She tossed her head ever so slightly as her eyes met his. "I'll take care of him for now."

He couldn't remember ever hearing more confidence infused into a sentence.

More lines began to ring until every light in the single row was lit. The buzzer went off again as two more people came in.

The man nodded in Jordan's direction and made himself at home on one of the chairs along one wall. The woman, apparently less familiar with her surroundings than the man, took a seat as well, perching awkwardly on the edge of the folding chair, looking as if she intended to take flight at the slightest provocation. Upon closer scrutiny, Jordan saw that she looked as if she'd been crying.

In the background, Jordan could discern what sounded like the arthritic rumblings of a battle-worn coffeemaker going through its paces, the water grumbling as it was being heated.

This was a far cry from the plush corporate offices

where he usually spoke to clients, Jordan thought as he took a seat at the desk opposite the couple that had come in first.

The second he put his full weight on it, the chair began to wobble beneath him. Caught off guard, Jordan grabbed either side of the desk to steady himself and keep from ignobly sinking to the black-and-white-checkered floor.

"Oh, and your chair has a loose wheel," Sarajane called out without even turning in his direction. She was busy taking down the names of the two people who had just entered. "I'd be careful how I sat down on it if I were you."

Maybe the woman was better suited to the fortune-teller's shop next door, Jordan thought as he nodded at the distraught couple.

He put on his most confident smile, the one he wore for the paying clients. He'd been told it put them at their ease. "How can I help you?"

Those were his last words for the next twenty minutes.

Chapter Three

Sarajane was prejudiced against good-looking men.

She had firsthand experience with the nature of the beast. Her opinion was built on a very firm foundation. Fresh out of college, ready to take on the world, she'd lost her heart to a good-looking man with a golden tongue: Rocco Santori, an incredibly good-looking man who was as shallow as a puddle on the pavement.

Lonely, needing love, needing to feel that soothing rush that came from being committed to just one man, she'd actually thought that Rocco was the man she could spend the rest of her life with. In addition to his looks, he was bright, intelligent and intent on making something of himself. She'd poured her heart into the relationship—and he had poured words. Lovely, beautiful words that had turned out to be empty, holding only air and precious little else.

She'd left him when she'd discovered that he was sleeping not only with her, but with two other women as well. Each of them had his promise of exclusivity to wrap their dreams around. It turned out that he was seeking to further his own career by using the women he slept with to his best advantage, to feed his ego, to make him feel invincible.

She couldn't get away fast enough. After that, she was wary, but her heart being what it was, she fell in love with someone almost a year later. Again, she was hopeful. Again she gave away her heart. Because Andrew Hopkins seemed different.

Seemed, but wasn't.

Like Rocco, Andrew belonged to the DDG Club, the Drop Dead Gorgeous Club. She came to the conclusion that all men who qualified for that club never bothered developing their personalities, or, more importantly, their scruples, feeling that their looks absolved them of ever having to trouble themselves with a sense of decency or morality.

In her experience, good-looking men didn't have to try as hard or do as much and they were still forgiven, still worshipped. All because of their looks. If they had the body to go along with that, almost any woman they encountered was lost.

Almost.

She now belonged to that small but exclusive group that could see right through the men of the DDG Club. Men like Jordan Hall, she thought, covertly observing him throughout the morning. Clinically speaking, Jordan was even better looking than either Rocco or Andrew had been. But it didn't matter. She'd had her shots. She was immune to handsome faces and biceps that rippled and butts that quarters could be bounced off. She'd take a homely, honest man any day.

If she were taking men, which she wasn't.

Mentally, she'd decided to retreat from the male-female battlefield for the present. Given that she was only twenty-five, she figured she had time to get back in the game—if she ever wanted to. And right now, that was doubtful.

Sarajane frowned thoughtfully to herself as yet another call came in and she picked up the receiver. She had fully expected Jenny Logan's high-profile brother to fade, to give up. It hadn't taken a stretch of her imagination to envision him backing away from his desk and heading for the door an hour after his arrival.

Especially after the Trans had arrived. Twelve people, all talking at once, a few lapsing into Vietnamese when they grew excited. One of them—the mother, she had discovered after joining the fray to try to untangle what was going on—had been the victim of identity theft, which, according to what the woman's oldest daughter had figured out, had begun over nine months ago. Mrs. Tran was being brought to court on all kinds of non-payment charges. There were bounced checks and staggering outstanding credit-card balances for items Mrs. Tran knew nothing about.

Trying to unscramble this information and make sense of what was going on would have tried the patience of a veteran, someone accustomed to dealing with ongoing chaos on a daily basis. Someone like Jenny. To someone like Jordan, who probably had never broken a sweat in his life or been made to struggle with any task, she just assumed, the matter would outdistance his ability to cope by several leagues.

Sarajane was amazed to discover that he did indeed have coping skills. More than that, he had an actual presence and could make himself heard above the noise, above the raised voices all competing for center stage with their version of the situation. As she watched, somewhat in awe, the way one did when confronted with a fish that actually possessed legs and could walk on land, Jordan called for order several times, refusing to continue until he finally succeeded in getting it.

The Tran family abruptly stopped talking and sat in respectful silence, waiting for Jordan to frame his questions. When he did and they began answering in unison, their voices blending in an eager cacophony of half words and sounds, Jordan called for order again.

Careful not to lean back in his chair, Jordan pushed it slightly back from the desk and scrutinized the gathering.

"Look, people, we're not going to get anywhere if you all keep competing with each other. Now appoint a spokesperson and just have that person talk. And if you hear that he or she is getting it wrong," he added, "raise your hand."

"Like in school?" the youngest Tran, a girl with the very Americanized name of Tiffany, asked.

Jordan nodded, a hint of a smile reaching his lips. Tiffany, Sarajane observed, instantly brightened, like a flower absorbing its first rays of the summer sun. "Like in school. Now, talk amongst yourselves and decide who is going to give me the particulars—and don't forget to consult with your mom." He nodded at the woman who was at the center of all this. A woman who, it was quickly established, spoke almost no English.

"She's not my mother, she's my aunt," Tiffany corrected him.

Jordan inclined his head, accepting the correction. "Whoever she is, it's her story to get out." A better idea came to him. Opening the middle drawer, he silently made a wish for paper. The lined yellow legal pad he discovered in the center of the drawer almost made him feel giddy. He took it out and handed it to the girl, who looked at him quizzically.

He tapped the pad and looked first at Tiffany, then at some of the other members of the family who were standing at his desk. Only the older woman and her husband were sitting. "Be sure not to leave anything out," he instructed.

He'd intended to get up and get himself a cup of coffee. He'd long since finished the contents of the container he'd brought with him. But instead, just as he was about to stand up, the phone on his desk rang. And rang.

Exasperated, he bit off a few choice words, saying them silently instead, and picked up the receiver. He did his best to ignore the Tran family who were huddled together on the other side of his desk, conferring and dictating to Tiffany.

"Jordan Hall."

There was silence on the other end. And then a female voice asked almost timidly, "Is this Advocate Aid, Inc.?"

Unfortunately, it is, he thought. "Yes, what can I do for you?"

The woman on the other end quickly launched into a tearful tale about not being able to locate her son whom the police had come and arrested several hours ago. When she'd called first one precinct, then another, no one would tell her where her son was being detained. Jordan made notes as fast as he could.

Out of the corner of his eye, he saw Tiffany had finished writing. She pushed forward the yellow pad and looked at him expectantly. He acknowledged her with a quick nod.

"I'll have to call you back, Mrs. Rodriguez," he said into the receiver. The words on the other end flowed more rapidly and freely. "Yes, yes, I promise. Ten minutes. Twenty, tops."

He became aware of Sarajane's presence at his elbow even as he was hanging up the receiver. Was she bringing him yet another person to deal with? He wasn't sure he could handle that right now. His cool was dangerously close to a meltdown. "What?" he bit off, looking at her sharply.

Sarajane didn't say a word. Instead, she silently placed a mug filled with coffee on the desk beside his elbow and withdrew.

Jordan knew he'd sounded like some curt jerk. He usually hung on to his temper a great deal better than that.

"Hey, I'm sorry," he called after her, momentarily forgetting that they were far from alone. Sarajane didn't stop walking or even turn around. But she did raise her hand over her head and made a little waving gesture, as if to brush away his words from the air.

For the time being, given the source, he took it as a supreme compliment.

The action continued nonstop. They were joined by Harry, who finally showed up sometime before eleven, and a woman named Rachel Sands, who

was on loan from somewhere for the week. Both
were lawyers. But Jordan quickly learned that Sarajane ran the show. It was Sarajane who directed the
almost constant influx of human traffic, organizing
them, getting them to fill out a minimum of forms
and seeming to prioritize their cases and degree of
need.

But even with Sarajane at the helm, the work was
daunting and constant. It didn't even let up long enough
for him to duck out for some lunch. Instead, after his
stomach had rumbled a number of times, he was given
a sandwich from a local take-out place. The wrapper
on the sandwich sported a logo: What's For Lunch? He
vaguely recognized it as belonging to a place he'd
passed in his search for Advocate Aid's office.

As with the coffee, Sarajane dropped the sandwich off at her desk. Jordan looked at her quizzically
as the man sitting before him continued with his narrative about losing his job after not giving in to the
sexual advances of his female boss. In response to his
silent query, Sarajane merely shrugged.

"Don't want you keeling over from hunger," she
told him as she walked away.

The next moment, he realized that the man had
stopped talking and was eyeing his sandwich.

"You going to eat all of that?" the man asked him
sheepishly, then added, "I haven't eaten anything
since yesterday morning."

He supposed skipping lunch wouldn't kill him.

Jordan pushed the sandwich over to the man who accepted it with profuse thanks.

Jordan realized that his eyes had slipped shut. He stretched out his legs beneath his desk, trying to shake sleep from his body. It was, in his estimation, one of the longest days of his life, including the time when he was nine and had broken his leg. His parents had been vacationing in Europe and it had been his nanny, a no-nonsense young woman from Australia named Emily, who'd brought him into the hospital emergency room. Because Emily insisted, he'd been kept overnight for observation. The TV in his room was broken and he'd spent the duration of the evening staring at a spider weaving a web in the corner of the ceiling. Time had dragged by like a sloth climbing up a tree with glue on its feet.

What he'd gone through today made him long for the serenity of the hospital room.

The moment he saw Sarajane flip the lock on the outside door, pulling down the shade that indicated they were closed for the night, he could have cheered. It was past eight. Darkness had long since descended on the city.

All he wanted to do was go home and pour himself a tall drink and forget about this place. "Is that it?" he asked rhetorically. "We're done?"

"For the day," Sarajane replied crisply. About to

walk right past him, she abruptly changed her mind and paused at his desk.

Jordan was in the process of shutting down his computer. Or trying to. The closing message seemed to have frozen on his screen and showed no signs of making good on its promise. He hit several keys that ordinarily sped up the process, but all he heard was clicking noises. The message continued to sit on the screen.

"What?" he bit off, feeling her eyes on him. All day long, he'd had the sense that he was being dissected and evaluated, part by part. Which was all right, except that he also sensed that in her estimation, he was coming up lacking. Which was *not* all right.

"Is there a problem?"

The cheerful note in her voice seemed out of place and irritated him more than he was willing to admit. Jordan reined himself in. "Can't seem to shut down the damn computer."

"Move aside," she directed, using her small body to edge him out of the way.

"It's all yours." Annoyed, he took a few steps back.

Taking his place, Sarajane proceeded to hit the same keys he had. The machine continued to be just as unresponsive. He felt oddly vindicated and then was surprised as she suddenly dropped down on her knees. As he watched, mystified, Sarajane crawled under his desk. She hit the switch on the power strip that his computer and monitor were plugged into, first once, then again. The first time she drained all the power from his computer and monitor, the second hit brought the electricity flowing back to them. Since she hadn't turned either the computer or monitor back on, they continued to remain dormant, ready to go through their paces another day.

The view from where he stood was nothing short of intriguing. The trials, literally and otherwise, of the day were mentally shelved as Jordan found himself staring at the woman's rather tight posterior muscles and the way her skirt strained against them when she reached.

He wondered if she worked out or if nature had been incredibly kind and generous to her. He had a feeling it was probably a little bit of both.

Sarajane wiggled back out again. He stepped to the side and offered her his hand to help her up. She stared at it for a second, then chose to use his desk for leverage and rose to her feet.

He decided her action said more about her than about him. "Independent to a fault?" he guessed.

She supposed that was one way to put it. Sarajane dusted off her knees, plucking out a staple that had gotten caught in her skirt. "That way, I don't get disappointed."

He shook his head. "Cynical attitude for someone so young."

She didn't particularly like the patronizing way he'd said that. "Practical," she countered, then blew out an annoyed breath.

He was astute enough to pick up on the warring vibrations she was giving off. "What?"

She was tempted to say, "Nothing," but that wasn't exactly truthful and the truth was very important to her. So she told him. "I was going to tell you that you did good."

Jordan studied her for a moment. Several times during the course of the day, he'd heard her being incredibly sympathetic and considerate with the people who'd crossed their threshold. Yet her tone now indicated that kind words did not come easily to her.

"But?"

"No buts," she told him. "You did good today. Better than I figured you would."

"Thanks. I think."

She began to walk away, then stopped. "By the way, Mary Allen is holding back."

"Excuse me?" After seeing more than twenty people, plus the crowd scene that comprised the Tran family, he was getting the names and faces confused. He tried to remember which one had been Mary Allen.

"She's holding back," Sarajane repeated. "She's not giving you the full story about the parental abduction charges."

Now he remembered. Mary Allen was the young single mother trying to regain custody of her two daughters. She looked like a little girl herself, hardly old enough to have children, especially not children aged seven and six. Talking to her, and watching her flirt with him, he'd gotten a sense that something was missing from her story. But he hadn't pressed her for it. By the time she had come to his desk, it was after four and all he could think about was getting out and going home to his wide-screen plasma TV and his comfortable sofa that didn't tip dangerously when he leaned back.

Walking away from his desk, he saw that Sarajane was moving about the rear of the office, shutting down lights and checking to see that computers were off. "You know her?" he asked.

One of the phones had the receiver off. Sarajane replaced it. She shook her head in response to his question. "No."

"Then how do you know that the woman was holding back?" He wasn't challenging her, he was genuinely curious.

She looked up at him, silent for a moment, as if debating whether or not he merited an answer. "You get a sense of things after a while. I can always tell when people are lying."

Jordan couldn't help being amused. His firm paid professional profilers good money to make judgments like that about jurors who were being selected. He doubted if Sarajane Gerrity had had any professional training in that field. "Can you, now?"

Something in his voice caught her attention. She looked up at him sharply.

"Yes," she replied firmly, silently daring him to argue with her. "I can."

But if she meant to bait him, he wasn't taking it. Instead, he nodded. "I'll keep that in mind."

Jordan watched as she returned to the small desk she presided over. Opening the lowest drawer, Sarajane took out her purse. Still moving, she extracted her wallet and took out a dollar bill and change.

He drew his own conclusions. Lengthening his stride, he caught up to her before she reached the back door. "Can I give you a lift?"

The other two people who had been in the office today had both left within five minutes of each other several minutes ago. He and this firecracker of a woman were alone now. It gave him a moment to study her, and think, again, that when her mouth wasn't barking out orders, she really was a rather beautiful woman.

"Provided that my car is still in the lot," he added, remembering his feeling about leaving the vehicle unattended.

She didn't care for his presumption. "How do you know I didn't drive here?"

He nodded at her hand. "You've got money in your hand and as far as I could see this morning, there was no valet parking."

There was no way this was going to get personal between them. They were just going to work together for the next three weeks and it was clearly up to her

to get the most out of him—professionally. She had
no desire to add another layer to that.

"Thanks," she said coolly, turning off the last light.
She stood in the doorway, waiting for him to walk
out. When he did, she locked the door and activated
the security code. "But the bus drops me off almost
at my door."

"So could I."

She was well versed in men like Jordan Hall. He
wouldn't drop her off at her door. He'd try to talk his
way into her apartment. That was about the last thing
in the world she wanted.

"Maybe some other time," she replied. And with
that, she pulled up the collar of her coat and walked
deliberately away, heading for the bus stop on the
next block—and away from him.

Jordan stood and watched her for a moment, then
told himself that she had no need or desire for a
guardian angel. And he had both when it came to that
drink he'd promised himself.

With a shrug, he turned in the direction of the
parking lot, hoping for a miracle. Trying to remember
where his insurance papers were, just in case.

Chapter Four

When he thought about it later, Jordan wasn't exactly sure why he took that route to go home. It certainly wasn't the fastest way to get out of the area and back to his own home ground. Maybe, after a day spent trying to be generally selfless and sympathetic for no other reward than the expressions on the faces of the people he'd dealt with for the last twelve hours, he'd begun to be predisposed to selfless acts.

Besides, there had always been a little of the defender of the fairer sex in him. He'd cut his teeth on books dealing with tales of chivalry dating back to the Knights of the Round Table.

Or maybe he'd just seen too many superhero movies.

Whatever the reason, Jordan decided, once he'd found that his car was still exactly where he had left it, with not so much as a single graffiti mark on it, that maybe he'd just drive by Sarajane's bus stop to make sure that the whirling dervish was all right.

Not that he expected her not to be. Jordan had no doubts that anyone foolish enough to try to take advantage of the young woman would get far more than he bargained for. She might appear to be soft and frail, but he had a strong feeling that she knew how to take care of herself. Her mouth alone should have been registered as a lethal weapon with the local authorities. Once she started talking, an avalanche of words would quickly bury the person on the receiving end, and they wouldn't stand a chance against her.

Jordan smiled to himself. Sarajane could probably have a great future in politics if she wanted to go that route.

Still, all arguments to the contrary, Jordan turned his vehicle left instead of right, just to assure himself that everything was okay.

The closest bus stop along the thoroughfare was located near the end of the next block. There was a streetlight situated several feet away from the rectangular sign proclaiming the area to be an official bus stop, but the bulb had gone out and apparently no one had gotten around to replacing it. Except for the light from the half moon, the area was deeply embedded in shadows. Looking, Jordan could barely make out two forms next to the bus-stop sign.

One, because of the diminutive height, had to be Sarajane. The other, taller, bulkier, obviously was a man waiting for the same bus. A man Jordan surmised Sarajane knew, given how close he was standing to her.

All right, he thought, she was okay and he was way overdue for that drink he'd been promising himself. Time to get home.

But when he reached the end of the block, intent on making a U-turn so he could take the shorter route back to his penthouse apartment, Jordan could have sworn he saw the man grab Sarajane by the arm.

And she didn't like it, Jordan realized. She was struggling.

Without thinking, Jordan stepped on the accelerator. The light was still red when he went through it, cutting across two lanes to reach the right side of the street, and Sarajane. The sound of brakes screeching behind him, coupled with the blast of a horn, told him he had narrowly avoided colliding with another vehicle. He didn't bother looking back. His entire attention was focused on the two figures at the bus stop.

Coming to an abrupt, skidding halt almost directly next to the pair, he knew he'd made the right call even before he got out of the car. Sarajane was definitely outraged, but there was no mistaking the trace of fear on her face.

He was out of his car like a shot, leaving the driver's-side door hanging open. "Let her go," Jordan ordered.

The man was even bigger up close. There were no whites to his eyes, only the disturbing reddish tint that came from hardened drinking. The smell of whiskey emanated from him and his clothes were rumpled, as if he'd slept in them at least once. The expression on his dark, stubbled face was malevolent, enraged by the intervention.

"Get your own ho," the man jeered, his expression growing uglier and more threatening by the moment. He looked as if his hamlike hands could easily smash to bits anything and anyone who roused his displeasure. "This one's mine."

"Think again." Pushing Sarajane behind him, Jordan put his body between her and her would-be attacker.

To her surprise, the man who had tried to drag her away from the bus stop released her hand. Breathing hard, she stared at Jordan's back. "What are you doing here?" she cried.

"I would have thought that would be obvious," he fired back, never taking his eyes off the brute before him. There was a quick movement. Jordan realized that the man had pulled out a knife. From the way he held it, the creep knew how to make it do his bidding.

"Back off," the stranger snarled. He followed the command with a particularly coarse label he affixed to Jordan.

Jordan's mouth curved in a humorless smile. "My

mother really wouldn't like hearing you call me that," Jordan said, his voice a steely calm that Sarajane found unsettling.

"You for real?" the other man jeered.

"My friends tell me so."

The answer was given at the same time that Jordan moved with a speed that took the other man completely by surprise. One minute he was apparently in control, the next he was on the ground, with the heel of a finely crafted Italian-leather shoe against his neck, his arm being yanked up and behind him. From the way he screamed, the pain from the movement was excruciating. Another barrage of words flew out of his mouth, ignited by the heat of his fury.

"I'm going to kill you, you son of a bitch!" the man raged, trying to get up. He screamed again as Jordan pulled harder.

"Get my cell phone out of my coat pocket and call 911," Jordan ordered Sarajane. "I'd do it, but my hands are full at the moment." He had both wound tightly around the mugger's arm, pulling it up and back as hard as he could. It was dangerously close to being snapped out of its socket.

Stunned, feeling like someone trapped in the middle of an action movie, it took Sarajane a moment to come to. "I've got my own cell phone," she told him.

She was arguing with him? Now? "I don't care if

you stand on top of the streetlamp and let loose with a Tarzan yell," Jordan ground out, "just get the damn police over here."

Sarajane realized that her hands were shaking as she pulled her phone out of her pocket. The fact that she'd been so badly affected by this lowlife bothered her a great deal. She took a deep breath, trying to steady her nerves.

Hearing nothing, Jordan glanced in her direction. She looked white, even in the sparse moonlight. "You all right?"

"Yeah," she said with more bravado than she felt. "I'm fine."

She'd lived in areas like this all of her life and never once had she ever come close to being assaulted or robbed. For the most part, she hardly ever gave her own safety a thought. It just wasn't one of the things she worried about.

But this put everything in a different light. This made her acutely aware of her own vulnerability, placing it smack on her doorstep. She didn't like it.

Taking another breath, she pressed the three keys that universally connected people to help. Someone answered on the fourth ring.

"Nine-one-one. What is your emergency?"

Sarajane turned away from the scene and Jordan. It was the only way she could get herself to speak.

"Hey, man," the assailant growled, "let me go. No need to call in the cops. This was a joke, just a joke."

"Then you'd better do something about your sense of humor," Jordan told him coldly.

The man tried to squirm, but with Jordan's heel in his neck, there was nowhere he could go. "You want money? I'll give you money."

"Save it," Jordan snapped. "You're going to need it for your lawyer." He glanced toward Sarajane to see how she was doing and yelled to her, "And we're not taking on his case."

Having given the pertinent information to the dispatch operator on the other end of the line, Sarajane ended her call. She turned around again as she returned her phone to her pocket. Her eyes narrowed as she looked at the man squirming on the ground.

"No way in hell," she affirmed.

The assailant tried to get up again and failed. "She was asking for it," he spat out. And then he screamed again as Jordan yanked his arm up higher.

Sarajane jumped at the bloodcurdling sound. She looked at Jordan, but his expression was mild, as if he'd done nothing more than just stretched his own muscles.

She couldn't draw her eyes away from Jordan. There was obviously more to the man than she thought.

"I'm taking you home, so don't bother giving me any excuses or arguments," Jordan informed her.

"I won't be giving any," she told him.

It was more than an hour later. The police had responded fairly quickly, arriving on the scene within ten minutes of her call. They took both her and Jordan's statements, then cuffed the would-be assailant, depositing him in the back of the squad car amid a hail of profanities. One of the arresting officers had told Sarajane that she would have to come down to the precinct to formally press charges tomorrow.

She'd nodded, promising to be there first thing in the morning.

Jordan took her gently by the arm and brought her over to his vehicle, now parked several feet away from the bus stop; one of the officers had asked him to move it.

He looked at her carefully, wondering if he should insist that they go to the emergency room of the closest hospital. "You sure you're all right?"

She wished he wasn't being so nice. If he'd lectured her, she could have rallied, could have had something to fight. But he had come to her rescue and was being her knight in shining armor. How was she supposed to rail against that? He didn't play fair.

Sarajane shrugged. "My faith in humanity's a little shaken up right now, but yes, I'm all right."

He opened the passenger door for her. "He didn't hurt you?"

She didn't sit down right away, afraid that her knees would start to buckle if she tried to get into the vehicle. She paused to pull herself together. "Maybe just my pride."

He didn't follow. "Your pride?"

Sarajane nodded. Her thoughts began to explore what might have happened if Jordan hadn't shown up when he did. But it was too painful to think about and she pulled back. Damn it, she was supposed to be independent and self-sufficient. "I should have been able to handle the situation."

She was being too hard on herself, and she definitely expected too much from herself. "From what I saw, it wasn't a debate. If it had been, you would have cut him to ribbons. But you're what—?" He looked at her. "Five foot nothing? That guy looked like he was at least twice your size."

She raised her chin defensively. "He was bigger than you and you handled him," she protested, then stopped abruptly. It had all happened so fast, she wasn't certain exactly *what* she had seen. "How *did* you handle him, anyway? I mean…"

Her voice had trailed off. She'd obviously realized that she was insulting him, Jordan thought, but he took no offense. The other man had been an animal and probably outweighed him by fifty pounds, if not more.

"Easy. I was one of those ninety-eight-pound weaklings as a kid." He continued to hold the door open for her. She took her cue and got in. Her knees were weak, but mercifully didn't collapse out from beneath her. He raised his voice as he rounded the hood to get to his side of the vehicle. "My father got me a personal trainer to build up my confidence and my body."

"Well, he obviously succeeded." Which was an

understatement, she thought. The man not only looked like a he-man but he behaved like one, too. A double threat, she mused.

"Lucky for both of us," he said, getting in. He closed his door.

Lucky.

The word echoed back to her in the recesses of her mind. She didn't know about that. Sitting inside the car, the doors closed, something softly playing on his radio, she found herself very aware of him. Aware of his presence, his body and the heat that he was giving off because he'd exerted himself with the mugger.

And she was more than a little aware of the fact that she wasn't as immune to good-looking men as she wanted to believe she was. But then, he had just saved her from things she couldn't bring herself to think about right now. He was the stuff that heroes were made of and her reaction to him was only natural.

It was time that she cut herself a little slack, Sarajane thought.

"By the way—" Jordan put the key into the ignition "—if I'm going to take you home—"

Okay, here it came, she thought, a wave of cynicism returning. The payoff. He was going to say something charming, all the while getting ready to take advantage of the situation he found himself in. And of her.

Sarajane braced herself, a sense of disappointment beginning to flow through her. So much for the accolades she had been heaping on his head.

"Yes?"

Why was she looking at him that way? he wondered. Was she in shock? *Should* he be taking her to the hospital? "I'm going to have to have your address."

"My address?" she repeated dumbly, staring at him.

He nodded. "You haven't given it to me. Unless you want me just to drive around aimlessly, hoping to get lucky."

He wasn't looking to take advantage, she thought, almost laughing out loud. God, when had she gotten so paranoid? The answer to that, she realized, was easy. Right after her misadventures with Rocco and Andrew.

She did her best to muster an apologetic look. "Sorry, maybe I am a little more shaken up than I thought."

"*Do* you want me to take you to the emergency room?"

Her eyes widened. "Oh God, no. I'm fine, really. Just take me home."

"Home it is," he agreed.

Damn but his voice sounded soft, kind. For two cents…

Too high a price to pay, she warned silently.

Sarajane rattled off her address, simultaneously telling herself to get a grip. At this point, it was a tall order. She felt as if she were a giant washing machine, her cycle stuck in spin. Everything inside her was all jumbled. She was surprised that she wasn't throwing up.

The trip to her apartment took next to no time at all, despite the cluster of traffic lights that were against him. As they drove, he tried to coax her to talk, which he found rather ironic, since during the course of the day, the sound of her voice was everywhere. But he was trying to put her at ease, to get her to distance herself from what had happened, at least for the night.

He discovered that contrary to his belief, she did have a car. She told him it was in the shop with a cracked engine block. Since that ran to over a thousand dollars, a sum she was only mildly acquainted with, it was going to be a while before she had enough money to bail it out. Until such time, she was going to have to continue to ride the bus.

"It's right there, that building in the middle of the block," she pointed out. She was still pointing to it as Jordan drove right by it. "What are you doing?" She twisted around in her seat, watching the building grow smaller again.

He squinted into the darkness. "Looking for a place to park."

She didn't see the need. She'd put him out enough already. "Why? You can just let me out here."

"Do I need to stop the car?" he asked her cryptically.

A hint of a smile curved her mouth. "If you slow it down enough, I can just jump out."

That was the kind of answer he figured she'd give. "Forget it. I'm walking you to your door, Sarajane."

He hadn't said her name up to this point. She liked hearing him say it.

Oh-oh, warning signs. Mayday. Mayday.

"You don't have to."

"Yes," he answered firmly, "I do."

Okay, he was giving her flack. She welcomed flack. Flack she could handle. It was kindness that undid her. She straightened in her seat, ready to argue.

"Look, what happened tonight has never happened to me before. Ever," she emphasized. "Lightning doesn't strike twice in the same place."

He gave her a look she found annoying.

"Slept through high-school science, did you?" he quipped. Seeing a space on the next block, he headed for it. "That's just an old saying to make little kids feel safer than they really are. Lightning most certainly does strike twice in the same place," he informed her. "Sometimes even more."

Where was this heading? She crossed her arms. "And you're going to do what—be my escort for the rest of my life?"

That was a tall order, one he had no desire to fill. He wasn't a masochist. "Why don't we take it one evening at a time? Just until you bail out your car."

In other words, forever, she thought, fighting a wave of dejection.

Parking, he pulled up the hand brake and turned

off the ignition. But instead of getting out, he turned to look at her. "Have you always been this bitchy, or did the mugging bring out the worst in you? Or is it me?" he added for good measure.

She sighed. He was right. She was behaving badly. That he had pointed it out didn't make it any easier to own up to, but she knew she had to. "I'm sorry. You're only trying to be nice."

Her apology instantly smoothed over all the waves she'd created. He smiled at her. "Well, at least you noticed."

Sarajane forced a smile to her lips, one she didn't feel. But he wasn't to blame for this. "I don't like being afraid."

"Most people don't," he agreed, then added, "unless there's something really wrong with them."

And then, suddenly, it just came out. The thought that had been drumming in her head, giving her no peace as it grew in size. Haunting her. It was a hard thing to swallow, given how she had always believed in the basic decency of humanity.

"Nobody else was stopping," she blurted out, doing her best not to cry. "A couple of cars went by and nobody stopped."

He saw that this bothered her. A great deal. He tried to make it more palatable for her. "They probably thought you were just having an argument with your boyfriend."

She shrugged. "Yeah, probably." But she really

didn't believe that. Pressing her lips together, she looked up at him. "Thanks."

He'd been wondering when she'd get around to that. Or if she intended to continue snapping at him because she hadn't been able to handle her own situation. "You're welcome. Glad I was there."

She offered him a small smile, one filled with the gratitude she felt. "Yeah, me, too."

He knew it cost her a lot to say that. That he sensed this about her surprised him. But then, he chalked it up to being a day of surprises.

Getting out of the car, he went around the front and came to her side. Jordan opened the door. "C'mon," he urged quietly, putting his hand out to her, "I'll walk you to your door."

Taking his hand, she slid out. "You could have been hurt, you know."

"It crossed my mind."

Actually, it hadn't. When he'd seen her being threatened, all he could think of was protecting her. More than his day in the office today, this brought home the way of the world that he preferred keeping his distance from. For the most part, he was securely insulated from the day-to-day struggles and dangers that existed just beyond his plush penthouse and even more plush offices.

He didn't much care for this world. It was too harsh, too heartless. He couldn't help wondering how people did it, how they managed to exist in a world that was bent on sucking out their souls at any given opportunity.

How did *she* do it? he further wondered, looking at Sarajane.

Opening the heavy iron-and-glass front door, Jordan took her into the building. There was an elevator in the small lobby, one that took its time arriving. It creaked ominously all five flights up.

"Why don't you move?" he asked suddenly.

"It has a certain charm," she countered.

He thought it best not to get into it with her right now. She was in a frail state, otherwise he doubted if she could have possibly said what she'd just said. This place wasn't charming, it was run-down. He wondered if Jenny knew of a better place for Sarajane, one that she could afford and that hadn't been built pre–World War II.

When they got out on her floor, the smell of disinfectant immediately assaulted him.

Sarajane saw him wrinkle his nose and felt another flutter in the region of her heart before she shut the sensation down.

"Janitor got around to washing the floors," she explained. She led the way to the end of the corridor. "Here it is…" she announced "…5 E. My apartment."

He nodded. "I'll wait until you get inside—and lock the door."

He said it so straight-faced, despite what had

happened tonight, she couldn't help smiling. "You take your responsibilities seriously."

He smiled at her then, and she felt something loosen in her kneecaps. Rigidly, she locked the same knees into place. There was no way she was going to let herself start traveling down a road to nowhere again.

"That's what makes them responsibilities," he told her.

Get out of here! a small voice ordered, fighting the onset of panic. Locating her keys, she opened the door to her apartment. "Well, good night. And thanks again." Impulsively, she brushed her lips against his cheek. The next second, she immediately pulled back, looking at him uncertainly.

The woman was nothing if not full of surprises, he thought for the second time today. He was almost looking forward to tomorrow. Almost.

"Lock the door," he instructed.

In an attempt at levity, Sarajane saluted, and then let herself in. She paused for a moment after shutting the door.

His voice came through from the hall. "Lock it."

Only after she flipped the locks did she hear the sound of his footsteps receding. And only *then* did her heart stop pounding.

Chapter Five

The squeak of sneakers running and pivoting on the highly polished gym floor competed with the loud whack of the ball hitting against the concrete wall. The smell of well-earned sweat permeated the small enclosed court, some of that sweat dripping into Jordan's eyes as he fought Eric for game point in their weekly round of racquetball.

Eric had been waiting for him at the fitness club, dressed and ready to play, when he'd arrived. Usually, Jordan was the first one there. Hurrying had put him off. He lost the first two serves, but his natural sense of competition had him rallying and now he was in the lead.

"So," Eric finally said, after a few words of aimless small talk had been exchanged. "How's it going? With Advocate Aid," he added when Jordan didn't answer.

"It's…interesting," Jordan finally said. Whether he drew out the sentence because he was trying to return a shot or because he was searching for the right word was unclear.

Eric spared him a quick look before breaking away to corner the ball and return it.

"Well, you don't look any the worse for wear. Your game's certainly gotten more intense." He took a long breath as Jordan lobbed the ball against the wall, sending it off at an angle that made him stretch to the limit. "Any connection?"

"With what?" Jordan wanted to know, never taking his eyes off the ball.

"With the cases you're handling these days." Jenny had always seemed consumed with helping each and every person who came through Advocate Aid's doors. But Jordan had always struck Eric as someone cut from a different cloth. Jordan was more like him. Competitive, accustomed to the best and to dealing with people who could pay for it. He didn't really see his best friend as capable of fitting into a place like Advocate Aid.

Jordan thought for a moment. It almost cost him the next shot. He supposed he was a little tense and that translated itself into the way he was playing.

"It might be because of the *amount* of cases I'm looking at," he admitted. "It just never lets up." From the moment the doors opened every morning, people just came pouring in. "I had no idea there were that many people who couldn't afford legal advice."

Eric laughed as he dove to return a serve and wound up crashing on the floor. He was up the next second, like an old-fashioned jack-in-the-box. "Think about what you charge an hour, Jordy. Not that many people can afford you."

That wasn't his point. He scrambled as Eric returned the play, making the ball's trajectory go high. Jordan leaped in the air to return it. "Yes, but there are less expensive firms than Morrison and Treherne," he pointed out.

Eric considered himself better versed in this world, thanks to Jenny, than Jordan was. "Hey, when you're trying to decide which bills you can put off paying until next month, a lawyer is just another luxury you really can't afford."

After four and a half days at it, Jordan begged to differ with Eric's assessment. "Listening to the legal bind some of these people have gotten themselves into, a lawyer is something they don't have the luxury of going without."

Eric tried to hide the fact that Jordan had him panting as he dashed for another return. The ball resounded loudly as it made contact. "Example?"

Leaping up, Jordan just caught the ball with the

tip of his racket, sending it back. "First day, there was this woman, Ada McCloskey, whose landlord was trying to evict her because he found someone else who was willing to pay twice what she was for her apartment. He raised her rent accordingly, she couldn't pay and he had served her with papers."

Breathing hard now, Eric chased after the ball, just barely getting it. He wiped perspiration off with the back of his hand. "So? Don't keep me in suspense. What did you do, Dudley Do-Right?"

Jordan ignored the jibe. "Had that Energizer Bunny who runs the office do a little research for me. Seems that the apartment was rent-controlled, a little fact that the client didn't know and the landlord conveniently neglected to tell her." He grinned, a feeling of triumph telegraphing itself through him. When he'd told her, the grandmother of three had thrown her arms around him and nearly cut off his air supply in her enthusiasm. "Bottom line was, she didn't have to move." As he said it, he whacked the ball even harder than before. Eric dove for it and failed to return the shot as he crashed to the floor. "She gave me a tea cozy."

This time, Eric lay where he was for a minute, gathering his breath. "A what?" he mumbled against the floor.

Jordan walked over to him and extended his hand. "A tea cozy."

Eric grudgingly took it and hauled himself up to his feet. "What the hell is a tea cozy?"

Jordan laughed. "I haven't figured it out yet, but it's what she makes. She has her own mail-order business, making and shipping them out."

Eric frowned, shaking his head. "No wonder she doesn't have enough money to get a lawyer." When he saw Jordan picking up the ball, he raised his racket in the air. "Uncle," he cried. Walking over to the side where he'd left his bottled water and a towel, he picked up the latter and draped it around his neck, dabbing at his forehead and face before looking at Jordan. "You're certainly on your game today."

Riding high on the victory, Jordan asked, "Best two out of three?"

Eric wiped the perspiration from his forehead again as he shook his head. "What do you think I am, a masochist?"

Jordan went to the opposite side of the room and picked up his own towel. He peeled off the navy-blue sweatband he wore. "I thought you liked this game."

"I do." Eric paused to drain half the pint bottle before continuing. "I just don't like losing and I don't know what it is about you today, but you're playing like you're possessed."

"It's tension," Jordan decided. For a second, he leaned against the wall and took a long drag from his own bottle.

"Tension?" Eric scrutinized his friend. "These people giving you trouble?"

The people were more or less interchangeable in

Jordan's opinion. He viewed them as an assignment, a challenge, pieces of a giant puzzle that he was solving. Dealing with them was different, but it wasn't actually what he found unsettling at the end of the day.

Jordan shook his head, screwing the cap back on. "Not the people."

Eric narrowed his eyes, puzzled. "Then what?"

Instead of answering, Jordan asked a question of his own. "What do you know about Sarajane Gerrity?"

"Who?"

Jordan laughed to himself. "I guess that answers that question."

Eric held his hand up to keep his brother-in-law from moving on. "No, wait a minute. The name's familiar. Let me think."

"She's the office secretary," Jordan prompted, although that word hardly began to cover what the woman did. She was more like the office manager. *And a Grade-A pain in the butt,* he added silently.

The light dawned in Eric's eyes. "The Energizer Bunny."

Feeling dehydrated, Jordan took another swig from his bottle. "One and the same. What do you know about her?" he asked again.

Eric shrugged, picking up his racket. "Not too much. Jenny introduced us once, at the last Christmas party," he recalled. "She's a looker." It was meant as a passing observation, but as he said the words, it dawned on him just what his friend's source of "tension" might be. "Is that it?" he wanted to know.

Jordan had no idea what he was talking about. "Is what it?"

"Are you putting moves on the woman?" He didn't wait for an answer, but, knowing Jordan, went with his assumption. "Jenny's not going to like that. She thinks the world of Sarajane, said the office would fall apart without her." He thought of Jenny's reaction to Sarajane's possible departure. She'd drag herself to the office. Jenny was nothing if not committed. "Don't you dare do anything to make that woman leave Advocate Aid, do you hear me?"

Jordan looked at Eric as if he'd lost his mind. This whole thing was just for three weeks. Two weeks and half a day, now. "Calm down, Eric. All I did was ask a simple question."

Eric had gotten good at reading between the lines. "With you, nothing is ever simple." He knew Jordan better than anyone, with the possible exception of Jenny. "And I know that look, that's the one you used to wear when you sighted someone who aroused your interest." Usually, it was diverting, watching Jordan operate. But not this time. "I'm serious, Jordy, don't mess with her."

Was that what it looked like to the outside world, to Eric? That he was "messing" with women? Jordan suddenly felt resentful of that image—

and weary. He'd gotten tired of the pursuit, of the game. It seemed somehow juvenile to him now. He realized that he wanted what his little sister had. What his best friend had. A mature, stable relationship. Someone to talk to, not just make love with.

"I have no intentions of 'messing' with her," Jordan replied. "I just wondered what her story was."

If that was all—which Eric doubted—there was a simple solution. "Why don't you ask her? As I recall, talking was not a problem for her." He grinned, remembering getting cornered by the woman while Jenny mingled. "Getting her to stop, though, was another matter."

The subject, Jordan realized, was making him uncomfortable. He didn't bother exploring why, he just changed it. "How's Jenny doing?"

Picking up his gym bag, Eric tucked his racket into it. A fond expression came over his face.

"Losing her mind already. You know how she is, she likes to be busy. Lying in bed watching television, is not her idea of a dream come true." He waited for Jordan to gather up his things. "I've hired someone to help take care of the house and a nanny for Cole until she's back on her feet." He chuckled. "Your mother came to help with the interviews."

Jordan pushed open the door, leading the way out. As they exited, another couple went into the room. "What asylum do I visit Jenny in?"

Eric laughed. His mother-in-law could be overwhelming. "Actually, she was pretty helpful. Seems she has a lot of experience hiring housekeepers," he deadpanned.

"That's because she used to send them packing in droves." It had seemed as if there was a new house-keeper or maid on the premises every few months. "So she was always interviewing new ones."

They walked down a long, brightly lit corridor, passing the weight room as they went to the locker area. "Jenny wound up hiring someone your mother found completely unsuitable."

"Nice to know some things never change." Jordan looked at his watch just before they reached the lockers. "I've got enough time for a quick shower and then I have to get back."

Other than when he was due in court, Jordan was usually very laid-back when it came to his personal time. "Sarajane keeping you on a tight schedule?"

He blew out a short breath. "At least I got off for lunch." Entering the locker room, they passed an at-tendant on his way out. "Monday I didn't leave the damn office all day. About all I have time for is a nibble before the next person comes to my desk with their tale of woe. How does Jenny stand it?" he wanted to know. "How does she stay so upbeat, dealing with this kind of thing?"

Eric arrived at his locker first. Stepping over the long bench, he began to work the combination lock. "She has me."

Jordan's locker was two numbers down from Eric's. "Like I said, how does she stay so upbeat?"

Eric's retort was suited to the locker room.

"You hair's wet," Sarajane commented twenty minutes later as she passed him on her way to her desk, her arms laden with files. He'd just walked in the door. "Is it raining?"

Having asked, she glanced over her shoulder to look through the front window, as if she didn't trust any answer he might give her.

Jordan bristled at her tone. He'd expected Sarajane to mellow toward him after he'd come to her rescue Monday night. Instead, it seemed as though the exact opposite had happened. She was even more cryptic, more demanding than she'd been the first day. If he didn't know better, he would have said she was trying to drive him away.

"I ran out of time at the gym and didn't dry my hair," he retorted. He couldn't help adding sarcastically, "I know how you value punctuality."

"You went to the gym?" She said it as if he'd just committed one of the seven deadly sins.

What the hell was her problem? "Yes, I've got a standing date with Jenny's husband for a racquetball game every Friday." He was standing toe to toe with her and he'd forgotten all about not letting her get to him. "Is that against one of your rules?"

She didn't like his tone and could feel her back

going up. These good-looking men thought they owned the universe. "Rules?" She didn't impose any rules, she just tried to keep everything running smoothly. "Did one of the balls hit you on the head? I don't know what you're talking about."

I'm talking about you acting like a crazy woman. He kept his comment to himself, opting for something less damning—and less insightful. "What I'm talking about is that you've been frowning at me all week, as if you didn't approve of anything I've been doing. If there's something wrong with the way I've been handling these cases, just say so."

She squared her shoulders and lowered her voice. "All right. You lack heart."

He'd certainly never been accused of that before. "Excuse me?"

Because they were garnering looks from the people who were seated near the front as they waited to be seen by one of the lawyers, Sarajane abruptly took his hand and marched to the back, bringing him to the tiny cubbyhole where she kept the office supplies and the vital coffeemaker. The entire area was hardly the width and breadth of a medium-sized closet.

Sarajane shut the door so that their voices, mainly hers, wouldn't carry. She told herself that she had no desire to embarrass him, only to change him.

"You lack heart," she repeated, saying the words more firmly this time.

That was probably one of the most ridiculous accusations he'd ever had thrown at him. "I'm a lawyer, not a handholder."

Her eyes narrowed in exasperation as she fisted her hands at her waist. Somehow, the movement had her getting even closer to him. "These people need compassion, they need understanding—"

"They need legal expertise," he cut in, "and I thought I was doing a damn fine job in that department." Blessed with a photographic memory, he'd been handling cases that were out of the realm of his usual field and recalling all sorts of old cases to draw on. "I'm not supposed to court them, I'm supposed to help them."

Was he really that thick? "Being compassionate *is* helping them."

He was finding Sarajane increasingly infuriating. The woman had no idea what she was talking about. "If they want someone to hold their hand, they can go to their friends, not waste our time."

Okay, she'd spell it out for this dolt. He might be a sharp lawyer in his field, but he was dull when it came to the attributes that counted.

"If you're compassionate, you find a way around the legal mumbo-jumbo that's ensnaring them and help them even if it isn't following the letter of the law."

"You're talking about bending rules, aren't you?" That wasn't the way things were done, except on TV programs in quest for high ratings.

Some things, she thought, irritated, were better

left unvoiced. It was less incriminating in the long run. "I'm talking about you being the last line of defense these people have."

"I got Mrs. McCloskey back into her apartment," he pointed out. He only remembered because he'd repeated the story to Eric.

Trust him to forget the salient point. "Because *I* found out that her apartment was supposed to be rent-controlled."

Which she wouldn't have done if he hadn't given her the assignment, he thought, struggling to maintain his temper. "Bottom line, she kept her apartment."

Her eyes were blazing. "No, bottom line is that Mrs. McCloskey *wouldn't* have kept her apartment if it had been left up to you to find a way to get her landlord to back off."

For the first time in his life, he was tempted to strangle someone. It was hard for him to think, to remain reasonable, with that perfume of hers filling his head. "What is it you want from me, Sarajane?" he demanded. "You want me to sit there and cry with them? Sorry, I don't cry. But I do have a hell of a lot of cases committed to memory that might just be able to help a few of these poor slobs—"

There, that was his whole problem, summed up in one word. "Hold it—hold it right there," she declared suddenly. "That's exactly what's wrong with your attitude." He looked at her, clearly mystified. "You think you're better than they are."

The woman was insane. How did Jenny work with her? "No, I don't," he told her tersely. The thought had never crossed his mind. He staunchly believed in equality, especially before the law. "I do, however, think I'm *better off* than they are." Maybe, in her mind, she'd gotten the two confused. Jordan gave her the benefit of the doubt even though, in his opinion, she didn't deserve it.

She tossed her head, sending her hair flying over her shoulder. From out of nowhere came the urge to run his fingers through the flowing mass.

"A circumstance of birth." She sounded almost haughty.

"No argument," he allowed. Then, in case she thought he'd done nothing but coast all his life, he added, "But I did work hard getting my education."

The man didn't know the meaning of the word *work*. Like all handsome men, he'd gotten by on his looks and, in this case, on his father's money.

"What? Waiting tables at night, dragging yourself in in the morning, trying to stay awake during classes, holding down a second job because the cost of tuition kept going up?"

Was she trying to make him ashamed of the fact that he hadn't had to struggle to make ends meet? It wasn't a sin to be wealthy. Only bleeding hearts thought so. He refused to be made to feel guilty about it.

"No," he answered, grinding out the word, "Studying."

She smirked. He probably hadn't had to do much of that, either. More than likely, he'd found a way to buy the answers to tests.

"Big deal."

He stopped abruptly, refusing to be dragged into this any further. It was like trying to shadow-box in the dark. "Why are you trying to pick a fight?"

Her chin went up, bristling at what she took to be an accusation. "I'm not picking a fight, I'm trying to make you a better man."

There was something about the way she looked when she became so incensed that aroused him. And goaded him on. Was it him, or had the tiny space shrunk a little more? "You'd be the first to complain."

She took in a deep breath, her chest hitting his abdomen. Damn his arrogance, he was lumping her in with his women.

"I'm not one of the bimbos you squire, Jordan," she informed him indignantly. "I'm not some plastic Kewpie doll. I'm a real person."

Something rippled through him as she drew in another breath, her breasts pressing against him again. "You are at that."

He had no idea how it happened. How the heated words that were being exchanged like gunfire could possibly have led him to take the next step. Granted the space between them was less than a breath and with each word she uttered, he found himself growing more and more annoyed. Growing more impassioned, something she was accusing him of being devoid of.

This was an argument about nothing. Nothing except the elephant in the living room: the very strong attraction he felt toward her and, he had a hunch, she felt toward him—most likely against her will.

But all that was reasoned out later, when he looked back at it and tried to find an explanation for his actions.

One minute he was engaged in a duel of words, the next there were no words. Others might be able to—and he had a feeling that Sarajane probably numbered among them—but as of yet, *he* had not mastered the ability to talk and kiss at the same time.

And the kiss took center stage.

Chapter Six

It was Adrienne McKenna who had introduced him to the world of kissing the day she'd pulled him behind his parents' pool house and put her lips to use in a way he'd never anticipated before. Adrienne had been the older woman in his life. She was twelve at the time and he was almost eleven. On that sunny, long-ago day, the degree of his attraction to the fairer sex heightened astronomically.

Even though it had been over twenty years ago, Jordan felt it safe to say that Adrienne McKenna had absolutely nothing on Sarajane Gerrity.

Jordan wasn't certain if he'd caught the overly energetic, incredibly opinionated woman unaware, or if, for that matter, she'd been any more unaware than he was about the pending event, but lightning had definitely struck the second their lips met. He might have unconsciously initiated it, but heaven knew that she had provided the fuel.

And then some.

Kissing Sarajane was every bit as exciting—and as mind-boggling—as he'd thought it would be. And now, as he deepened the kiss, simultaneously digging his own grave, every inch of his body came alive.

Alive? Hell, that was an understatement. He felt as if he were on fire and the temperature all around him was rising by the mega-second.

Jordan ran his hands along her back, pressing her to him, savoring the sensation, the moment, even as he began to lose touch with reality.

A second before it happened, she saw it coming. Sarajane had meant to pick her hands up and block any contact before it occurred. Meant to, but somehow she couldn't quite seem to execute the simple movement. Couldn't quite lift her hands up to wedge them against his chest and perhaps even to push him back. Instead, they remained at her sides, paralyzed by what she saw in his eyes.

And then, the next moment, all of her limbs almost seemed simultaneously to go limp as he kissed her.

And all sorts of explosions were going off inside her.

The kiss was far more than just breathtaking, it was life-force-taking. It was a struggle for her simply not to get sucked in and obliterated.

And then she rallied, because she knew if she didn't, she'd go down for the third time without ever having broken the surface even once. She was *not* about to be a casualty of a card-carrying member of the DDG club, not if she could help it. Taken in twice—once by Rocco, once by Andrew—the third strike would have been a permanent out and she was not ready to sit out the game of life for the rest of her years. Not yet, by God.

So, summoning all the fire, all the verve, that she had within her well-supplied arsenal, Sarajane suddenly rose up on her toes, wrapped her arms around Jordan's neck and kissed the invading enemy back. Hard. With every fiber of her being.

And, as sometimes happened with these things, succeeded in dangerously rocking her own world at the same time.

Meltdown seemed imminent and only moments away. She could feel the heat traveling up and down her body, all but singeing her very core. She wanted him. Knew she wanted him. And knew, above all else, that she couldn't allow that to happen.

Ever.

Survival instincts kicked in and Sarajane managed to slip her hands between Jordan and herself, although how was a mystery since there was less than enough space available there to fit in a buffalo-head nickel flattened by a runaway semi.

Jordan felt her fingertips pressing hard against his chest. He moved his head back at the same time that he drew in a long breath, then let it out again. To his dismay, it sounded shaky.

Clearing his throat, he loosened his arms from around her torso. But not without a sudden surge of regret. It took effort to summon the smile to his lips. "Well, glad we cleared that up."

Sarajane stared at him. He was kidding, right? They hadn't cleared up anything. What they had done—what *he* had done—was muddy up the waters. A lot.

How was she supposed to work with him now that she had almost gone up in smoke because he'd kissed her? And what made it even worse was that he knew it, damn it. He knew it.

"I could have you up on harassment charges." The desperate words all but leaped out of her mouth in self-defense against the emotions that were flying and colliding all through her like drunken butterflies without a flight plan.

To her mounting anger and embarrassment, she saw a grin forming on his face

"Where's your evidence?" he asked mildly. "Anyone who was watching us a few minutes ago would say that you were the one who pulled me into this room, not vice versa," he pointed out, his expression now the picture of innocence. "So, if anyone can cite harassment in this case…"

Jordan let his voice trail off, the wicked smile on his lips displaying a sense of confidence he didn't have at the moment. But then, his insides still resembled a burnt offering.

Stunned, Sarajane stared at him. He wouldn't dare—would he? It hit her that she didn't know. She knew very little about this man other than what she'd read in the papers and what his doting sister had told her—two very opposite sides of the spectrum.

"What?" she demanded angrily.

He had her going for a second, he thought. The sense of triumph that he'd expected eluded him. "I was just pointing out the obvious," he told her. "You were the one who took my hand and dragged me in here."

Her shoulders snapped back, more rigid than a surfboard. "I didn't drag," she retorted.

He felt tempted to remain here, in this small space with her, and see where the escalating heat would eventually take them, but that kind of behavior belonged to someone still in college, possibly law school, but not a man who had passed the bar and pleaded the cases of men and women whose faces were on the pages of *Fortune 500*.

"I'd love to continue this debate," he told her in a voice that she found absolutely infuriating and patronizing, "but we have people out there waiting for us." Just as Sarajane took a step toward the door, he added, "How about we continue this later? Say, perhaps over dinner?"

Other women might melt all over him like chocolate over a hot fudge sundae, but she wouldn't. "In a pig's eye," she snapped.

"I was thinking of some place a little more spacious, say, a restaurant." He said it as if the idea had just come to him, as if his entire life hadn't been conducted in the grip of lust. "I happen to know this intimate little place—"

"I just bet you do." Without sparing him a look, Sarajane pushed past Jordan and marched out the door—before she did something stupid like pulling him into her arms again.

The air within the outer office was by no means brisk, or even fresh, but after the heat that was blazing inside the supply room, stepping outside made her body feel as if it was enveloped by the breeze of a new spring day.

He was right on one count. They *did* have work to do, especially her. Work that refused to do itself no matter how much time she gave it.

About to head to her own crammed desk, Sarajane stopped short when she saw Alicia Juarez. The other woman made eye contact and began to walk in her direction.

Alicia was a nurse at the Children's Connection fertility clinic, and Advocate Aid often gave the clinic free legal advice, handling its paperwork and, on occasion, untangling messes that arose. Its help had been invaluable three years ago, during that awful period when the organization was besieged by one scandal after another. First there was that series of unfortunate fertility mixups, and then there was that black-market baby ring that had somehow attached itself to the organization by preying on the needy character of Robbie Logan, himself a victim of childhood kidnapping.

The tempests looked as if they were about to be unleashed again after the *Portland Gazette* ran a story about a teenage father whose parental rights had been completely ignored, first by his girlfriend, then by the Children's Connection who took his baby and passed it along to an adoptive couple without consulting him. The story made it sound as if the father, one Thad Sanders, was desperate to gain custody. In truth, he just wanted to be bought off, but no one paid attention to that. It was the scandal they were all eating up.

Although trouble at the organization was the logical reason for the young nurse's unexpected appearance, Sarajane had an uneasy feeling that the barely subdued look of fear on Alicia's face had nothing to do with that.

Jordan and her own unbridled reaction to him momentarily forgotten, Sarajane quickly circumnavigated a desk and hurried over to the woman. Alicia was just a little more than two years older than she was, and they were friends, even though the fast pace of both their lives sometimes made it impossible to touch base as often as they would have liked.

Sarajane put her hand on Alicia's arm and felt her friend trembling. Her concern increased. She tried, however, to seem cheerful, hoping that would bring her around. "Alicia, hi. What are you doing all the way out here in no-man's land?"

"Miss, I've been waiting here for over an hour," a burly man with day-old stubble declared, suddenly catching her arm. "That means that I'm ahead of her."

"I'm sure you are," Sarajane replied sweetly, suppressing the urge to tell him to sit back down. "But she's not here on business. Are you?" she asked, lowering her voice as she directed the question at the woman whose long, black hair and golden complexion she had always envied.

A feather would have sent her to the floor when Alicia nodded her head. "I am."

"Get in line, honey," the man directed haughtily. "It's first come, first served around here."

Before she could open her mouth with some soothing platitude, Sarajane heard Jordan cheerfully inform the man, "Ah, democracy at work. But not, I'm afraid, in your case." His smile widened as he placed himself between Sarajane and the heavyset would-be plaintiff. "The young lady's invoking Sadie Hawkins's rules."

The man looked at him, clearly confused. "That some kind of legal mumbo-jumbo?"

Jordan's face was never more serious. "You might

say that." He turned toward the office manager. "Sarajane, why don't you show your friend to my desk?"

"Legal mumbo-jumbo my foot," Sarajane said in a whisper between lips that were hardly moving as she passed him. "You're citing a character out of a comic strip, aren't you?"

Following, Jordan allowed himself a smile. He supplied the name of the actual strip. *"Li'l Abner,"* he told her. "Hasn't been around for decades. You're full of surprises, Sarajane." And then he momentarily shifted his eyes toward the back of the office, to the supply room. "But then, we've already established that."

She opened her mouth to say something, only to shut it again when nothing came out.

Jordan leaned over, whispering so that only she could hear. "You're blushing, Sarajane."

"It's hot in here," she informed him tersely. It was a lame comeback and she knew it, but she couldn't just let the comment go.

His smile only deepened. "My thoughts exactly."

And then he straightened and transformed right before her eyes from a Casanova to the personification of a professional attorney as he turned his attention to Alicia Juarez.

Jordan gestured toward the empty chair before his beleaguered desk. One week into working here and the cavalcade of papers surrounding his ancient computer had doubled, albeit neatly so because he had a thing about neatness, even in the midst of chaos.

"Please, have a seat, Ms.—?" He paused, waiting for the woman to fill in the name.

"Juarez," she told him as she nervously made contact with the chair, perching rather than sitting. "Alicia Juarez."

"Ms. Juarez," he repeated, covertly looking at her left hand to see if he should stretch her title out and insert an *R* between the two letters. The hand with its neatly trimmed, short nails was devoid of any jewelry, making her legally single in his eyes. "What can I do for you?"

"Alicia works for the Children's Connection." Sarajane told him when Alicia hesitated.

Sarajane was still hovering, he thought. It was a habit of hers, one that, he'd noted, he was on the receiving end of more than the other two lawyers in the office. Was it because he was still new in her eyes, or because she had this overwhelming need to control and micromanage everything she could?

Whatever the case, he could do without having her breathing down his neck, judging every move.

"I can take it from here, Sarajane," he assured her, turning toward Alicia. "I've done some legal work for your organization," Jordan told the young woman gently, hoping to help her get her narrative started.

To his surprise—and Sarajane's—Alicia shook her head. "This isn't about the Children's Connection." The words seemed to come tumbling out in a heap, as if glued to one another.

"It's not?" Sarajane interjected before Jordan could say anything.

Jordan spared her a glance that was less than patient, even though his voice remained controlled. "I've been here since Monday. I think my training wheels can come off, so you can—" He didn't get a chance to finish.

"It's about Joe," Alicia said suddenly, looking at Sarajane.

"Joe?" Jordan asked. "Is that your—" He was going to ask Alicia if Joe was her significant other when Sarajane interrupted again.

"Joe is her older brother."

They were back to sparring again, Jordan thought. Funny, for a moment back there in the supply room, he really thought they had connected. Clicked. Which meant that they should have been moving on to another stage of their relationship instead of reverting back to where they had been that very first morning—and again the morning after that—despite the fact that he had rescued her from the mugger, and then had taken her, the following day, down to the precinct to file charges against the man. That should have put them on a different footing. And yet it hadn't.

It seemed that with this woman, any progress made was only temporary, destined to fade from memory as they returned back to step one over and over again. It was like being stuck in some kind of science fiction time loop. He could only go so far before he found himself yanked back to the very beginning again.

It bothered him more than he liked.

"Thank you," he replied coolly, then turned his attention toward the angst-ridden young nurse sitting on the other side of his desk. "Why don't you tell me in your own words exactly what it is that you need me to do."

"I need you to represent him—my brother," she added needlessly. He saw that she was nervously twisting her fingers together in her lap. "He's in jail right now, and I can't make bail," she lamented. "And the court-appointed lawyer he has wants him to accept a plea bargain, but he won't do it."

Jordan nodded, doing his best to be sympathetic, at least for Alicia's sake. She seemed genuinely distressed by what she was telling him. "And why is that?" he wanted to know.

Alicia took a breath, as if she was fortifying herself before saying, "Because he's innocent."

Ah, the battle cry of two-thirds of the prison population, Jordan thought. He couldn't help the wave of cynicism that washed over him. But he kept the harsh words to himself. The young woman sitting before his desk with fingers that were all but knotted together looked too upset to have that little fact callously pointed out to her.

So instead he asked, "And what is it that your brother's innocent of?"

Alicia let out a ragged breath. It was as if words failed her.

"Take your time," Jordan coaxed gently.

"But not too much," Sarajane pleaded as another two people walked in.

It was bad enough conducting what were supposed to be private interviews out in the open like this. He didn't need an audience of one not so secretly critiquing every word he uttered.

"Sarajane, why don't you show those two people where they can sit?" he instructed more than suggested. She didn't like him telling her what to do, he guessed. But more than that, he saw her reluctance to leave Alicia's side. "She'll fill you in later," he promised, instinctively knowing that Sarajane would give Alicia no peace until she'd heard everything.

Grudgingly, Sarajane walked over to the newcomers.

Jordan leaned in closer, lowering his voice. "All right, what was your brother officially charged with?"

Alicia pressed her lips together. He noticed that they quivered a little. She was struggling not to cry, he thought. As he waited, his eyes never leaving her face, he reached over to the side and opened the drawer where he'd seen Sarajane stick the box of tissues. He placed them on his desk before Alicia.

"The official charge is grand larceny," she told him, then tagged on quickly, "but he didn't do it."

"And that's what we'll tell the judge," he assured her, never once allowing his lips to curve at the simple, almost sweet naïveté she was displaying, "but I'm going to need a little more to offer than that."

Ordinarily, the story should come from the accused, but he thought he'd let himself find out just what he was in for before going to talk to her brother. He could tell by the look on Sarajane's face that there was no way he could even entertain the idea of turning Alicia down and survive, at least not intact.

"Why don't you tell me what I'm going to be up against?"

"Then you'll do it?" Alicia asked eagerly. "You'll take on my brother's case?"

Because human contact was essential and telegraphed comfort, he took her hand in both of his and smiled as he told her, "That was never in question."

From across the room, Sarajane saw Jordan smiling at her friend. And she felt something stirring inside her belly she neither liked nor wanted to let into her life. But the sharp sting of jealousy needed no invitation. It came unannounced, unbidden and all the more hoary for that as it quickly burrowed right in, making itself at home.

She sighed and realized she might be facing her third strike after all.

Chapter Seven

Alicia's hands were folded before her on his desk. Only close scrutiny on his part allowed Jordan to see that her hands weren't folded so much as tightly gripped together, as if that was the only thing that was keeping her from falling apart.

Alicia took a breath and began, her voice hardly more than a whisper at the start, then taking on strength and breadth as she continued explaining her brother's predicament to him.

"Joe is—was," she amended ruefully and there was a flicker of anger in her eyes as she was forced to change the word, "the chief mechanic for Hell's Raiders, the successful motorcycle racing team," she interjected, in case he had never heard of the name. Few outside the racing world had. "I don't know all that much about them, but I do know that he's put in a lot of extra hours, hours he wasn't paid for," she emphasized, "working with their engineer to build this new kind of engine that uses alternative fuel. The modifications made the motorcycles run faster— and cleaner. The fuel he used was even safer for the environment," she added with feeling.

"Might be just what we need," Jordan commented, his voice soothing, his words meant to urge her gently to get to the heart of the matter.

"It certainly was what the team needed," she told him. "They tested the engine prototype and it performed even better than they'd originally hoped for during the initial trials. Everyone was excited. They were sure this would put them in the running for the lead this racing season."

He could hear her tone drop just at the last word. "But?"

The enthusiasm faded from her eyes. She pressed her lips together. "But then the plans for the engine went missing."

"What about the prototype?" He knew people who could work miracles just by looking at an example. If they had the engine, they could work backwards and write down the plans. Problem solved.

But Alicia was shaking her head. "It vanished," she answered quietly.

"And they arrested your brother because—?" he asked, leaving the end of the sentence open for her.

He could see how reluctant she was to fill in the blank. "Because Joe was the last one who worked on the plans—and the engine—before they went missing." She drew herself up. "I know this looks bad for him, but he didn't do it," she insisted with feeling. "Mr. Hall, my brother is a single dad with two kids to raise—Joey junior and Lia. He works very hard and he really loves those kids." Her eyes were passionate as they pleaded with him. "He wouldn't do this to them."

He banked down the urge to comfort the woman. That wasn't going to help her. Right now, he needed to play devil's advocate, make her aware of all the possibilities. "Did you stop to consider that he might have done it for them?"

Alicia's soft brown eyes stared at him. "I don't understand."

He knew it was filial love that was blinding her. But no one on the jury was going to be related to Joe Juarez. They were going to be looking at the facts. And at what was obvious.

Jordan mapped it out for her. "Well, considering the state of affairs these days with the price of gas going through the roof, everyone's looking for an alternative fuel and a better, more efficient engine that will run on it. And there's your brother who just happens to have both in his hip pocket."

Alicia splayed her hands on his desk, leaning forward. Incensed at the mere suggestion that her brother was a common thief. "Joe wouldn't do that," she insisted. "He's not like that."

Everyone was like that when the chips were down, Jordan thought. "When your brother went to work for these motorcycle racers, he signed an agreement, didn't he?"

Her eyebrows drew together in confusion. "What kind of an agreement?"

"That any idea he might come up with that had anything to do with enhancing or augmenting their vehicles actually belonged to his bosses." He'd seen it happen time and again, brilliant inventors made to surrender their life's work because they had accepted someone else's terms in order to get funding to get them started.

She thought for a moment, trying to remember. "Yes, but—"

There was no but in this case, he thought. It wasn't fair, it wasn't right, but that was just the way things were.

"Think how it must have felt to your brother, to actually have come up with something that would put him on the map, make him a lot of money for his family, and then to know that he would never reap any of the benefits that might come of that because he signed his life away to his employers." His eyes held hers as his voice dropped lower, but the underlying intensity continued to build. "Think how frustrated that must have made him feel, to stand back and know someone else, not his children, would get the money, that someone else would get all the fame that rightfully belonged to him."

"No." She shook her head with feeling. "Joe's not like that," she cried again.

It must be nice, he thought, to have someone believe in you that much. Outside of Jenny when it came to Eric, he'd thought such women were pretty much wishful thinking on the part of males. Obviously not.

"Then he's a saint," he told her matter-of-factly.

He saw the disappointment wash over her face. "You sound just like his lawyer."

"No," he corrected patiently because there was method behind his being so harsh. "I sound just like the plaintiff's lawyer. That's what they're going to say at the trial. They're going to point out the obvious to the judge and the jury. They'll hang their whole case on it and right now, from where I sit, it sounds pretty convincing. Are you sure you still want to fight this and not just tell your brother to accept the plea bargain that he's being offered?" He did his best to look sympathetic, to her plight if not to her brother's. "Maybe you should try talking to him again."

He watched as Alicia raised her chin proudly. "I don't have to go to talk to Joe, I know exactly what he'll say. That if he accepts the plea bargain, he's telling the whole world that he did it. But he didn't do it and he wants his kids to know that."

Noble, Jordan thought. And very foolish. The man was playing Russian roulette with his life. "Even if it means the difference between being out in two years or ten? If not more." It all depended on the judge they drew. "How are his kids going to feel then, with daddy doing a long haul in jail?"

Her expression told him that she preferred to look on the positive side. "But if you take the case, Mr. Hall, my brother won't have to do any time. You'll prove he's innocent." Her smile was warm and filled with hope. "I know your reputation," she told him. "Sarajane told me you were going to be working here, taking Jenny's place and I immediately looked you up. Your bio on your firm's Web site says that you've never lost a case."

No, he hadn't. But the words in themselves were a heavy burden. Because he'd never lost a case, he had a great deal of confidence in himself. However, because he'd never lost a case, there was a part of him that was holding its breath, waiting for that first time to finally occur. That shoe to drop. Hoping it wouldn't, yet fearing it eventually would.

This was no time to give in to idle mental specu- lation or, worse, self-doubt, he told himself.

Besides, if she had that much faith in him, the least he could do was to cloak himself in more of the same and do what he did best for her.

Win.

He nodded. "All right, Ms. Juarez, I'll take your brother's case."

"Oh, thank you, Mr. Hall. Thank you," she cried.

Jordan doubted if he'd ever heard that much gratitude infused in a voice before. When Alicia opened up her hands, he saw that her fingers were almost red. She'd been clenching her hands that hard. *Praying that hard?* he wondered.

And then he saw her open her purse and begin to rummage through it. Was she about to show him some kind of proof she'd been holding back? More likely, she was going to show him pictures of her brother, or better yet, her brother's children. But he was already on board, there was no need for that.

He was about to stop her when she said, "I don't have much," Alicia dug further into her purse, then surprised him by taking out a fistful of dollar bills. "But I can pay you on the installment plan. From now until the end of time," she added with a rueful smile.

He felt oddly touched. Jordan gently pushed her hand back.

"This is a free legal-aid clinic," he reminded her. There couldn't have been more than thirty, forty singles there, he mused. Did she moonlight as a waitress? Were those her tips?

"Yes, but you don't come free," she countered. It was obvious that she really had done her research, up to and including what he charged by the hour. More than she made in a week, he was certain.

"I do when I'm here," he assured her. "House rules."

"But what if the case continues after you have to go back to your firm?" She glanced around to see if she could locate her friend, but failed. "Sarajane said you were only here for three weeks."

"We'll work something out," he promised. Jordan gave her an encouraging smile for good measure and then leaned forward across his desk, pushing a pad and pencil toward her. "Now, if you tell me where they're holding your brother, I can go see him this afternoon and start the process."

Alicia wrote down the name of the jail where her brother had been held since the arraignment, then pushed the pad back to him. Impulsively, she leaned forward and threw her arms around his neck for a moment, relief and hope all mingled together in the one quick gesture. "I don't know how to thank you."

Jordan smiled, more to himself than to her. She had no idea what kind of a leading line that was, he decided. The woman was genuinely naïve—and sweet. "We'll think of something—after your brother's free."

Alicia rose to her feet. She took a deep breath. "I like the sound of that. You were right—" she addressed the words to someone behind him "—he is good."

He really didn't have to turn around, but he did anyway. Sarajane was behind his chair. Her sudden appearance really didn't surprise him. Since he'd gotten here, she'd been doing that, materializing like Casper, in this case, the not-so-friendly ghost.

He was, however, a little surprised by the testimonial. "You said that?"

"I believe in being supportive and encouraging whenever possible," she informed him crisply, her expression flat—until she looked at her friend.

Sarajane's lips curved then in a wide smile even though she was a little hurt that Alicia had kept this from her even as she had asked about Jordan. She'd never put the two together, that Alicia was asking not out of curiosity, but out of need. As friends, she'd just assumed that if something was wrong, Alicia would have told her. Obviously, she'd assumed wrong.

She had to be getting back. Alicia pulled her purse to her.

"I won't take up any more of your time," she told Jordan. "But that's my cell number." She pointed to what she'd written at the top of the page. "If you need to ask me anything, if you need anything at all," she stressed, both her gratitude and her concern etched on her face, "just call, night or day."

He nodded, folding the paper and tucking it into his pocket. "I'll be in touch," he promised as he watched the nurse walk away.

"In touch, or touching?" Sarajane asked with more than a tad of sarcasm, her voice low so that it would go no further than the small space around Jordan.

He looked at her without bothering to hide his

amusement. "Testy," Jordan commented. "After all, she's your friend."

"Exactly." Sarajane looked at him pointedly. "And very vulnerable right now."

Even though there was a roomful of people around them, he took a second to look at her. His expression gave nothing away. "Not like you."

His words halted her in her tracks. Sarajane didn't know if he was being serious, or if he was just saying that sarcastically to irritate her.

For a split second, it almost felt as if the man could see through her. Through the bravado she kept tightly wrapped around her, straight down to her two failed relationships. When he'd kissed her, had he somehow detected—

No, that would be giving him too much credit, she thought. The man wasn't a superhero with extraordinary powers, he was, from what she'd heard, an exceptional lawyer with an equally exceptional as well as insatiable taste for the ladies. She needed to keep that in mind at all times—and to keep her emotions, not to mention her lips, in line.

"Not a bit like me," she agreed.

With that, she quickly turned to the next person who was waiting and indicated that she take the chair Alicia had just vacated.

Jordan sat down again, bracing himself. The impatient man who had tried to huff and puff some attention his way was now sitting next to Harry's desk, bending his ear. Sarajane was bringing him a woman whose eyes were red-rimmed from crying.

It was going to be a long afternoon.

The frown etched lines into Robbie Logan's thirty-seven-year-old face as deep as the words he was reading on page three. The air of despair permeated the office from which he lovingly ran the Children's Connection Day Care Center.

He knew that Nancy had told him not to let the stories get to him. His wife had even gone so far as to tell him she didn't want to see any copies of the *Portland Gazette* in their house.

But not buying the newspaper wasn't going to change anything. It wasn't going to make the stories go away.

It seemed like nothing really made the stories go away. They'd abate for a while, then return in another form. To plague him.

Robbie sighed, scrubbing his hands over his face. He pushed the newspaper away. It fell on the floor. For the time being, he left it there.

Why now?

Why again?

A hopeless frustration filled him. He was trying so hard to do the right thing, to be the right person and it wasn't as if it was easy, not after everything he'd been through. But it seemed to him that every time he thought he was finally going to make it, finally get on track, life had a way of throwing obstacles in his path, derailing him. Making it harder for him to surmount the wreckage that he'd always felt was his life.

It hadn't always been this way, he tried to remind himself, there'd been good things, even in the beginning. Especially in the beginning. But at times it was hard to hang on to those good memories, especially when there were so many bad ones waiting to cancel them out, dark clouds overtaking the white.

It wasn't all that long ago that he was known as Everett Baker, just another worker at the Children's Connection, an adoption agency and fertility clinic located in Portland and heavily funded by the charitable contributions of the Logan family. Everett Baker, the adopted son of Jolene and Lester Baker, two of the most worthless, twisted people who had ever walked the face of the earth.

Adopted son.

The term mocked him. A more accurate description would have been kidnap victim. Lester, trying to appease his shrew of a wife, had kidnapped Robbie one day while he was playing with a friend, taking him from the loving home he'd had and convincing him that his parents didn't care about him. That they were glad to be rid of him.

What Lester and Jolene did was brainwash him, make him feel unwanted, unloved. Unworthy. They'd tortured him emotionally until there was nothing left of the boy he'd been.

Nothing but that one last shred of integrity. It took a while for it to surface, buried beneath hurt and resentment, qualities that allowed him to be duped by Charlie Prescott, the man who was really behind the black-market-baby schemes and the IVF mix-ups. Charlie preyed on him, preyed on his insecurity and pretended to be his only friend, all the while determined to use him to help with the kidnappings and the blackmail he was trying to pull off in order to feather his nest.

But in the end, that shred of integrity won out, causing Robbie to thwart Charlie's plans and turn him in to the authorities.

Nancy had been the reason for that. She'd seen in him the man he had the potential to be. The man he could have been if he hadn't been kidnapped. She was the one responsible for his finally having the courage to seek out his family, people he'd felt himself unworthy of, and tell them who he really was— their long-lost son and brother. Nancy had been his source of strength then.

Nancy was his source of strength now, but that didn't change anything. That awful story was digging up everything in his past, laying the blame for the supposed oversight in the Sanders baby case at his doorstep. Whoever was writing this story was calling him a former baby kidnapper. They were implying all sorts of awful things, making him out to be a monster instead of the victim that he actually was.

He knew what that meant. There'd be trouble at the Children's Connection. Donations would be pulled, people would stop coming. And he would be the one to blame for that.

Or so it would look.

He'd survived his kidnapping, survived the unfair charges that had been brought against him the first time around; he'd been proven innocent. He'd managed finally to feel worthy of being who he actually was: Robbie Logan, oldest son of Terrence and Leslie. Granted it wasn't easy to erase all the years that had gone by, but he was taking baby steps in the right direction.

But all that was going to stop, to change, because of this latest set of allegations.

This latest set of lies.

A man could only take so much before breaking and he had taken more than his share. Robbie sighed, pulling over a large sheet of paper. He picked up a pen and began writing.

He owed it to Nancy to get them away from all this unfair, undeserved attention. God knew she deserved better even if he couldn't seem to merit it himself.

After a few minutes, he put down the pen and looked over the words he'd hastily scribbled on the back of a form letter the department had sent out when the story first broke. Ordinarily, he would run something of this nature past Nancy before putting it into play. He never made decisions without consulting Nancy. She was the more level-headed one. But this time, he'd made his own decision.

Because of Nancy.

She wasn't one to complain, but he knew this had to be hurting her. Hurting her because she loved him—God only knew why. And hurting her because she was associated with him and people talked. He didn't want anyone thinking badly of his Nancy.

So he signed the letter, even though his heart ached as he did it. Dropping the pen again, he rose from his desk. He needed to tender his resignation from the Children's Connection now, before it got any worse.

Before he lost his nerve.

Chapter Eight

"Ready to go?" Jordan asked Sarajane as he watched her lock the front door.

For his part, he'd shut down his computer twenty minutes ago, when he'd begun ushering the last supplicant out the door. That had taken about ten minutes, and the dialogue of the last eight he couldn't really remember. But now, finally, after what seemed like a full thirty-six hours, it was the end of the day.

More than that, it was the end of the week and he really felt like celebrating that. One week down, two left to go. It couldn't happen soon enough for him. This place, he'd decided, was nothing if not a real downer. He'd never had to deal with so many downtrodden people in his life. People whom life seemed have to either forgotten or run over. People who were turning to him—and Advocate Aid—as their last hope. God knew it was hard not to let it get to him after a while.

One or two of the people he had seen this week had almost, albeit unintentionally, made him feel guilty about the silver-spoon life he'd led and, in fact, was still leading.

Almost, but not quite.

After all, it wasn't as if he was living off his parents' money the way he knew that some people in his circle did. He *worked* for a living. Worked damn hard at times. Whenever a case demanded it, he put in long hours to see it through to its ultimate satisfactory outcome. If his clients were the kind who could afford to pay top dollar for the best, well, that wasn't exactly his fault now, was it?

More like his good fortune, Jordan mused, packing up the notes and the file he was going to be reviewing sometime this weekend, during a lull. Joe Juarez's file. The lawyer who'd been appointed to handle the man's case had been more than happy to relinquish everything to him.

Obviously Tim Seger was someone else who wasn't exactly thrilled about handling pro bono cases. He'd gone to see the lawyer after he'd had his rather quick first interview with Joe Juarez this afternoon. There'd been a flicker of recognition in the attorney's eyes. After Jordan had introduced himself, the other man had been almost nauseatingly eager to be of any help. Jordan knew it was because of the firm he was associated with. That, and his reputation. Seger had confided that he hoped someday to work for a firm like Morrison and Treherne, if not that actual firm itself.

In a pig's eye, Jordan mused. His firm hired only the top of the graduating classes from the country's best law schools.

And being the best had landed him here, he thought darkly.

Yes, he wanted to celebrate getting out of this dingy, claustrophobic storefront office by stopping at one of his customary haunts to help eradicate the stench of desperation that seemed to be hovering around him, thanks to the people he'd interacted with.

How the hell did Jenny stand it? he wondered. How did she manage to maintain her good mood, not to mention her sanity?

But then, he supposed that was what made her Jenny.

Jordan thought of just mumbling goodbye to Sarajane and ducking out. But he supposed playing the part of a selfless do-gooder had gotten to him a little. He couldn't just let the woman go off on her own and stand at that damned bus stop again, not after what had happened on Monday. After running for two days, her vehicle was in the shop again.

That's what came of buying a used car, he thought.

The damn thing had been pronounced "fixed" by what he could only assume was an idiot of a mechanic. She'd driven it to work Tuesday afternoon only to have it refuse to even attempt to start on Thursday evening. She'd probably maxed out her credit card to pay for it, too. He'd remained with her, waiting for the tow truck. The truck had taken her car back to the mechanic where it now currently resided, just this side of limbo.

Sarajane crossed back to her desk and got her purse. The dialogue, she thought, was undoubtedly useless, but she felt honor bound at least to try to talk him out of taking her home. Besides, she really didn't like feeling indebted to him.

"You don't have to do this, you know." Closing the deep bottom drawer with her knee, she slipped her purse strap onto her shoulder.

He was already on his feet, heading for the back door. "Please, Sarajane, it's Friday. I don't feel like going through this dance again. You need a ride, I have a car, it's not that far out of my way." Following her out, he waited until she locked that door and turned on the security system.

She turned to face him, turning up her coat collar at the same time. It was unusually brisk out tonight. "Far enough."

Habit, as unconscious as it was automatic, had him taking her elbow and directing her toward the parking lot. "So I'll earn a merit badge that much faster."

She stood beside the passenger door as he unlocked it. "You could never qualify for a Boy Scout."

He held the door opened for her—his very action, he felt, a contradiction to the kind of behavior she was obviously ascribing to him. "And why not?"

She got in and waited until Jordan had rounded the trunk and gotten in on his side. "Because you're much too wicked."

Jordan stopped turning the ignition key and looked at her. "Excuse me?"

"Wicked," she repeated. "As in Casanova. Romeo. Lothario. Don Juan. That kind of wicked," Sarajane clarified.

He laughed, shaking his head. This time he completed turning the key and his sports car hummed to life. Shifting from the brake to the accelerator, he eased his baby out of the parking spot. He'd surveyed it quickly before getting in and been relieved to see that it was still free of marks or dents. He counted that a victory.

Jordan spared her a glance before getting on the main thoroughfare. "Spend a lot of time reading, do you?"

Her eyes narrowed. Was that a put-down? "As a matter of fact, I do."

The expression on his face said he'd expected as much. What was his problem? "Maybe you should try living life instead."

Sarajane shot him a scathing look just as they

squeaked through another almost-red light. "I *am* living a life. Every day when I walk through Advocate Aid's doors, I live these people's dramas, their heartaches. Their fears."

That was all just convenient rhetoric, he thought. She was hiding behind her work. Hiding from life by getting entangled in someone else's. He wanted to find out why.

"I meant something a little more personal in terms of living, Sarajane. Something that would require you to bring down that barricade you like to keep up around yourself, something to make you let your hair down. Be a woman."

Who the hell did he think he was? she thought angrily. Other than a driver who liked living on the edge of a traffic violation. They whizzed through another yellow light turning red.

"You should talk," she jeered.

She liked, he'd noticed, to turn arguments around, to flip the tables on him whenever possible, taking the center spotlight off herself and turning it on to him. "Excuse me?"

"Hell, Jordan, if you were any more removed from the people who come in, they'd have to come to see you in the next state."

Granted he had trouble relating to these people, but he thought he'd hidden it successfully enough. Besides, she'd said something else to him that first evening. Was that to placate him then, or was she just insulting him now? "I thought you told me that I was doing a good job."

One of the things that her work here had taught her was how to say things without flinching and giving away her true thoughts. One run-in with an abusive father and husband who'd come looking for his family had taught her how to lie with the best of them.

She raised her chin now and put that talent to use, saying dispassionately, "I lied."

He was quiet for a moment. So quiet that she thought maybe the conversation had abruptly terminated, ending in her favor. She should have known better.

"You always lash out like that when someone gets close to the truth?" He wanted to know just as they reached a red light. He was forced to wait behind a canary-yellow VW bug.

He was giving himself a hell of a lot of credit. "Meaning you?" she asked coldly.

She watched the side of his mouth. She could see it curve and felt something ripple inside of her. Sarajane dug her fingernails into her palms to divert her attention.

"Unless there's someone else in my car besides the two of us," he replied.

Sarajane didn't like his high-handed tone, didn't like what he was implying and most of all, didn't like the ripple in the pit of her stomach. Survival instincts kicked in.

"Stop the car," she ordered.

Looking through the windshield, Jordan glanced quickly around to make sure that the order hadn't come because he was about to run over something, or that he'd missed seeing some sort of an illegal incident going on in the vicinity.

But neither was the case, so he continued driving.

"Stop the car!" Sarajane cried again, infuriated because he wouldn't listen.

When he still didn't pull the car over to the curb, she reached for the handle and tried to open the door on her side.

Seeing what she was up to, Jordan kept one hand on the wheel as he lunged over as far as he could, the seat belt digging into his shoulder, to stop her. He grabbed her by the arm and yanked her back, the sudden movement breaking her connection with the handle.

"Are you crazy?" he demanded angrily. He was going forty. If she jumped out of the moving vehicle, she'd get hurt.

"Probably," she shot back, angry at being stopped. Angry that he thought he could exercise control over her. "I should have my head examined for getting into the car like this."

And what made him persona non grata all of a sudden? He'd been working his tail off to keep the caseload from growing.

"What are you—some kind of bleeding heart who

blindly chants mantras thought up by some feeble-minded jerk who like to stir up trouble? Rich is always bad, poor is always good, is that what you believe? Well, maybe you could try looking at the facts sometime," he told her, his words heated, his tone cold. "My family donates a hell of a lot to those charities you're so hot for and my sister has given up her whole life in order to help people who aren't on the social register. And all of them—my parents, my sister—are usually flying under the radar. Nobody even *knows* the kind of sacrifices they make. They don't do it for the limelight."

She didn't like having that sort of sentiment associated with her. "I don't believe rich is bad," she informed him quietly.

Turning down the next block, he shrugged. "Well, it's a start."

Oh, but there was something about the pitch of his voice, the tilt of his head, that made her want to scream. So she fired a comeback at him. "I do, however, believe that you're being held prisoner by the power and the allure of recognition and money."

Now that *really* made no sense. "Then what the hell am I doing here?"

When she blew out a breath, burrowing her back deeply against the seat, the small blast of air ruffled her bangs. "As near as I can figure it, driving me crazy."

There was something in her voice…Jordan shifted his focus, interested. Curious. And maybe, just maybe, a little aroused. He glanced in her direction as he slowed at another light. "Why? Why, Sarajane? Why am I driving you crazy?"

She folded her arms protectively before her, her body language warning him to back off. "You just are."

But he shook his head. "Not good enough."

And she had a feeling he would keep at it until she gave him something. So she did. "Because you remind me of somebody."

Now he was *really* curious. "Who?"

She didn't even want to say his name. "Somebody I don't want to be reminded of."

Too bad, he thought. She was the one who'd opened this Pandora's box. Fascinating him.

"Who?" Jordan pressed again. "Somebody who hurt you?" he guessed when she said nothing.

Sarajane stiffened in her seat, her shoulders as straight as a steel girder. She was all set to tell him to go to hell, that it was none of his business and she wasn't about to edify him with any kind of an answer.

But somehow, that wasn't what came out. "Someone I used to be with."

Jordan barely got through the next light in time. His attention was definitely shifting. "In the biblical sense?" he wanted to know.

The very thought of her "being with" someone unsettled him—and set his imagination moving into areas he knew would infuriate her. But then, she had the body of a goddess, even though she tried to hide it beneath clothes that were one size larger than she needed.

Instead of answering, she glared at him. Which provided him with an answer in its own way.

"And I look like this guy?" He made what he felt was the logical leap.

No, you're better looking. Which is the problem. She pretended to look in his direction, but her eyes barely swept over him. "In a general sense."

And just what the hell did that mean? "I need more details."

She stared straight ahead through the windshield as she said, "He was good-looking."

When she said nothing more, he looked at her incredulously. "So that's it? You're just going to go around and take potshots at all the men you think are good-looking?"

She noted that he didn't just place himself into that category exclusively. He'd made it sound as if it was a large group strictly of her choosing and according to her own guidelines. She supposed that gave him points. At least he wasn't conceited the way Rocco had turned out to be. Looking back, she realized that Rocco could never pass a mirror without at least a slight pause of appreciation.

This had gone too far, she thought suddenly. She was softening toward Jordan. Not what she had in mind, she thought. "Look, we're almost there. I can walk from here."

In response, Jordan hit the button that locked all four doors simultaneously. He wasn't through asking questions yet. "How did he hurt you?"

Sarajane bristled instantly. "I didn't say he hurt me."

Did she really think he was that obtuse? "You didn't have to."

She'd had enough of this. "Look, save the interrogation for the courtroom, Jordan." And then she realized that he'd thrown her off her game and she hadn't asked the one question that actually mattered. "How did your interview with Alicia's brother go?"

Jordan had left the office at four and she'd fully expected him to go home after talking to Joe Juarez. If she were being honest, she hadn't expected him actually to go to the county jail, but he had. And when he'd returned a couple of hours later, she was even more surprised. Silently, grudgingly, she had to admit that he was working out better than she'd first thought.

"He seems on the level," Jordan allowed.

His first impression of Alicia Juarez's brother was that the man was a fighter. He'd spent most of the initial short interview looking into Joe Juarez's eyes, and he saw a man who had been through a great deal, but who somehow still believed that, in the end, life would be fair to him. He believed that he was going to walk out of the cell a free man, his name cleared. As he spoke about what had happened to him, Joe had displayed just the right amount of anger and hope to hook him, Jordan thought.

Sarajane looked at him, suddenly hopeful for her friend. "So you can get Alicia's brother off?"

It wasn't nearly that simple. Right now, everything appeared to be tilted against them. "I didn't say that."

She interpreted his inflection. "So you *can't* get him off?"

As she watched, she saw what amounted to a Cheshire-cat expression form on his face. "I didn't say that, either."

Sarajane sighed, exasperated. He wasn't letting himself be pinned down either way. She absolutely hated secrecy of any kind. It wasn't as if she was going to post any information that came her way on the Internet, she just had an overwhelming need to know. Everything. If you knew everything, then there were no surprises to catch you unaware.

"God, you really are a lawyer, aren't you?" She shifted in her seat, the belt straining against her shoulder. "Okay, exactly what is it that you *are* saying, Jordan?"

"That it's not going to be easy proving he's innocent. For one thing, he has no alibi." For another, everything pointed to his stealing the plans. It just seemed too convenient, too neat. Nothing was ever that cut-and-dried, which in turn made him smell a setup.

She frowned. "Most people don't go around anti-cipating needing an alibi for themselves." To prove her point, she asked, "For instance, what were you doing at eleven o'clock last night?"

He didn't even have to stop to think before he answered. "I was in bed."

"See?"

"I didn't say alone," he added quietly just to see her reaction. Jordan watched in fascination as her complexion changed from ivory white to a pinker shade. Embarrassment? Or something else?

"We're here," Sarajane announced tersely, pointing toward the building in the middle of the block. "Please unlock the door."

"I didn't say I was alone," he repeated. "But as a matter of fact, I was."

So, what was he doing? Baiting her? Trying to get a reaction from her? Just what was he trying to prove, anyway? "I don't care."

The look on his face told her that he didn't believe her protests. "Could you say that under oath?"

For two cents, she'd push him out of the car—except that it was his car. "No more games."

"Okay." Jordan eased his vehicle into a space that was almost directly in front of her building and then pulled up the hand brake. "No more games." But instead of unlocking the doors as she'd expected, he leaned over the console and framed her face with his hands. "I was never into games anyway."

She felt his breath on her face, felt her pulse suddenly go haywire. "I…have…to…" The words dribbled from her lips, abruptly stopping as they went nowhere.

"Yes?" he coaxed helpfully, his lips barely inches away from hers. Her pulse was beating so fast, it was close to breaking the sound barrier. "You have to—"

Her mind was a blank, a complete blank, burned away by what was going on inside of her. Bedlam. Bedlam with a bonfire.

"I forgot," she whispered the confession.

Were she more lucid, she would have been embarrassed, or even angry that Jordan had this kind of an effect on her. Were she in more control of her faculties, she would have died before she allowed him to see that he was scrambling her brain. But the pure truth of it was, he *was* scrambling her brain.

This was even worse than with Rocco or with Andrew. Despite the suspicion and distrust she brought with her to the table, she couldn't seem to use it as a weapon, couldn't seem to set up a barrier to hide behind. Not that it probably would have done any good, she realized ruefully. If there was a barrier, she'd be leaping over it to get at him.

But pride demanded at least some sort of a rally, some sort of a show that she hadn't been reduced to a mindless puddle of desire.

"So," she asked, "are you going to kiss me or stare at me all night?"

A lesser man would have been put off by the flip remark. But then, a lesser man wouldn't have seen through it. And he did. She was scared, he realized. She'd been burned and she was scared. He could understand that. Moreover, right now, he could even relate to it a little, because part of him was a little unnerved at the level of attraction he felt every time he was in this woman's presence. Every time words were exchanged. It was almost completely over-whelming—and unsettling.

Just for now, because he felt like celebrating, because he had survived the week and only had two more to go, he didn't bother thinking about why he found her so attractive, or that feeling so might be dangerous to his self-preservation. He just went with the flow.

"I'll opt for the kiss," he told her, his voice soft, caressing her.

And his lips found hers.

Her mind shouted *Mayday* just before it completely ceased to function.

Chapter Nine

It was, Sarajane realized, as if she were drowning in chocolate. Dark, sweet, thick, rich chocolate. And oh, the rush that overtook her was almost not to be endured. The world around her had gone into slow motion and disappeared.

The second kiss was even better than the first.

She lost her breath. Completely and utterly. She found herself gasping just to draw in enough to sustain her.

Sarajane had never experienced anything like this before. Not from a kiss. Lovemaking was a different story, but Jordan wasn't making love with her—

Or was he?

They didn't actually have to be lying in bed, their bodies naked and tangled, in order to make love. Sarajane was one of those people who believed that someone could make love to you with their eyes, with their hands, with their lips.

Like now.

Oh, she was sinking fast.

Within another moment, she was going to completely forget all the promises she'd ever made to herself about getting involved, about setting herself up to be abandoned emotionally and physically, and surrender to this man with the lethal mouth that was to die for. The hunger within her was growing at an alarming rate.

Battling a huge wave of reluctance, Sarajane managed to separate herself from him, pulling back as far as she was able.

Only then did she realize that the ache she was feeling around her midsection didn't have so much to do with the longing a woman felt when she hadn't made love for a very long time as it did with the transmission shift that had been digging into the lower portion of her ribcage.

Jordan was looking at her and for the life of her, Sarajane couldn't read what was in his eyes. Amusement? Longing? The knowing look of a man moving in for the kill on a sure prey?

One coaxing syllable out of his mouth and she knew she'd succumb, that her last shred of resistance would dry up and just blow away. She had to say something first, squelch any hope that something was going to happen tonight—no matter how much she wanted it to.

"I have a roommate."

"I don't."

The two words echoed within the interior of the vehicle, buzzing around her head like a honey bee.

So this was temptation, she thought. Temptation in its rawest form. She knew Jordan was asking her, without actually putting it into so many words, to come to his place. To go home with him and be with him in every sense of the word.

Every fiber of her being screamed: "Let's go!"

Only her brain, that tiny fragment that was maddeningly given to common sense in times of crisis, shouted, *"No."* As much as she wanted to be with him, as much as she wanted to make love with him until she figuratively and maybe literally came apart at the seams, Sarajane knew that her brain was right and that everything else was wrong.

Wrong never looked so good to her before.

"You earn more money than I do," she said, sucking in air. Trying to find herself amid the ruins. Trying desperately to think so that she could mount a defense. Because if she gave in, there would be hell to pay in the morning.

Maybe sooner.

Jordan looked at her, bemused. Up until this moment, he'd thought that whatever else Sarajane was, she was sharp. This had come out of left field and just hung out there without a perch, without a link. Was she resentful of the fact that he was a successful lawyer? And how did that figure into anything?

"What does that mean?"

Oh God, she was going to gasp if she wasn't careful. Very slowly, trying to look as if she were thinking instead of trying to fill her lungs with air, she drew in a breath.

"That's why you don't have a roommate," she told him, "because you earn more money than I do and don't need anyone to share expenses with."

He knew that she understood what he was trying to convey, but he played along. "I didn't say that because I wanted to discuss economics."

"I know why you said it," she quickly interjected before he could use that golden mouth of his to say something seductive and reduce her to a puff of mindless steam.

Jordan had always known when to retreat, when to be the epitome of a gentleman. And maybe, just maybe, Sarajane was right to block this. Maybe they shouldn't spend the night together. Who knew what he'd be like, coming out of the other side of this encounter? As it was, he felt as if his mind was being played with. Maybe acting on his feelings was not in his best interests at the moment.

He smiled at her. The lady was something else, though. "I take it you're turning me down."

She would have thought that he would have tried to push, at least a little. But he just sat there, smiling at her. Melting her bones and looking complacent about it. Obviously the man wasn't nearly as into her as she was into him.

Well, what the hell did she expect? she upbraided herself. The only thing she represented to him was another conquest, nothing more. If she turned him down, well, he undoubtedly had an endless supply of women to turn to for consolation. If not her, then someone else tonight, right?

She told herself she should be proud that she wouldn't be numbered among his bimbos, that she stood apart from the crowd.

Somehow, it didn't really help.

Sarajane blew out a breath, wishing she'd taken the bus, muggers notwithstanding. "I take it that doesn't happen to you very often."

He shrugged casually. To say something self-effacing here would be a lie. And he had a feeling that Sarajane Gerrity didn't suffer lies, or liars, easily. "I don't keep a tally, but no, not really."

Her mouth curved in a smile that could only be termed ironic. "I guess that makes me unique."

He looked at her and suddenly she felt herself all but being hypnotized. And certainly drawn in. "You don't need to turn me down to be unique, Sarajane."

She held her breath, expecting him to make a move after that. It was, after all, the perfect opening, the perfect line.

But he didn't.

At least, not in the way she'd anticipated.

Jordan nodded toward the sidewalk. "C'mon, I'll walk you to your door."

Go home, Jordan. Go home before I make a fool of myself. She shook her head. "It's not necessary."

He put his own interpretation to her reluctance. "Don't worry, Sarajane, I won't try to push my way in if that's what you're afraid of." His easy smile broadened. "Knowing you, you're probably versed in some ancient art of self-defense that would have me flat on my back in less time than it takes to talk about."

She didn't. She'd always meant to take a course in self-defense, but somehow, the timing had always been off. There never seemed to be enough hours in the day. And now, more and more of her time was eaten up by Advocate Aid. That left no time for learning the fine art of tossing an attacker over her shoulder.

If she had, she suddenly thought, there would have been no need for Jordan to have come to her rescue Monday night. She could have taken care of that mugger on her own.

"I'm not afraid," she assured him, leaving intact his assumption that she did know self-defense. Better safe than sorry, she reasoned. Turning in her seat, she unbuckled her seat belt and then opened her door. Or tried to. "Jordan, you need to open the locks," she told him.

"Sorry."

He hit the appropriate button on his armrest and all four locks popped open again. He noticed that she lost no time getting out of the car. She would have probably dashed into the building, he mused, leaving him behind if his legs weren't so much longer than hers. He caught up with her at the building's entrance and pulled open the glass-and-wrought-iron door for her.

The elevator was on the ground floor and they got in. As they rode up to the fifth floor in the antiquated car, Sarajane filled the air with rhetoric, jumping from topic to topic like a frog leaping from one burning lily pad to another. Her mouth seemed to move faster than he thought possible for a human being. If she took a breath between sentences, he wasn't aware of it.

The second the elevator door opened, she made a beeline for her apartment. Did he make her that nervous? he wondered. He supposed turnaround was fair play. She made him nervous as well. An odd sort of nervous that he both relished and held suspect.

"Okay, well, here we are," she announced needlessly since this was where he'd already dropped her off the other night.

"Yes," he murmured, stopping her cold by moving

a strand of hair away from her face, tucking it behind her ear. She could feel the tip of his finger glide, ever so lightly, along the outline of her ear. "Here we are."

Her breath stopped in her throat. She needed him to back away. Now. Before something happened. "Jordan, this isn't going to work."

His smile went straight to the pit of her stomach. How did the man *do* that?

"Work implies labor." He paused for a moment to lean his forearm along her shoulder, toying with her hair. Messing with her mind. "This wouldn't require any labor at all."

It felt as if there was a lump in her throat as big as a cattle car. She had to concentrate to push the words out. She felt like a drowning man too far from shore to make it back, praying to snag a line. "You know what I mean. There's no future in this."

She made it sound much too serious. He wasn't interested in forever, only in now. "I've learned that you have to live in the moment. The future will take care of itself."

"That's not a very stable approach to life," she pointed out.

"If *stable* is another word for *stodgy* or *in a rut,* then you're right. My approach leaves you open to a lot of possibilities, to trying different things." Then, because it was just not in his nature to push, even when he knew he had the advantage and even though he'd never wanted to more than he did right now,

Jordan stepped back, creating a pocket of air between them. "See you Monday, Sarajane. Sweet dreams."

Sweet dreams? she thought as she opened and then closed the door to her apartment rather loudly. *Torrid* dreams was more like it. That was what he'd doomed her to, she thought, kicking off her high heels before she took another step into the apartment. She'd come this close to jumping the man's bones.

This close, she thought miserably. And he knew it. She knew that he did.

So what? she silently demanded the next moment. All that meant was that she was a normal, red-blooded woman. Anything that happened between them, that she *wanted* to happen between them, was motivated by nothing more than just pure sex.

She refused to think of it as anything else.

What she needed was a cold shower, Sarajane decided. Maybe an ice-cold shower despite the fact that the landlord was being stingy with the heat again and it was cool in the apartment. Why hadn't her roommate turned up the heat?

For that matter, where was her roommate?

"Missy," she called out. "Missy, where are you?" There was no answer. She raised her voice. "Are you here?" After her shower, she was going to want to talk, or watch a movie, or do *something* to get her mind off the sexy attorney who had almost undone her. "Missy?"

Her voice echoed back to her, being absorbed by

the drapes and the furniture. The light was on in the kitchen, but it could have been left on from this morning. Missy had a habit of forgetting that, unlike sunlight, artificial light was not free.

She made her way to the kitchen anyway. And found herself staring at a note secured to the refrigerator with a magnet that announced: My house was clean last week, sorry you missed it.

"Sara," the note read. Sarajane frowned. Missy never liked calling her by her full name, said it wasn't sophisticated enough. Only good manners had kept her from saying that *Missy* sounded like a nickname belonging to either a spoiled heiress or a stripper. "I'm taking off with Clint for the weekend. See you Monday—maybe. XOXO Missy."

Wow, Sarajane thought as she turned away, that had been close. She'd really dodged a bullet that time. What if she'd invited Jordan in for a drink?

Come for the drink, stay for the sex. Well, not this time, she assured herself.

The victory felt hollow.

She really needed that shower.

Sarajane began to head to the bathroom, shedding clothes as she went. Trying vainly to get Jordan's face out of her head.

It wasn't until much later that she realized that she'd used the words *this time*—which meant that she was in a state of anticipation.

* * *

Jordan's cell phone rang in his pocket just as he was about to secure his seat belt and start the car. Releasing the belt, he took out the phone and flipped it open without bothering to look at the name. It was dark inside the car and right now, he welcomed the opportunity to talk to anyone but a telemarketer. He needed his attention diverted from the woman he'd just left behind. The woman who was raising his body temperature, apparently against both their wills.

"This is Jordan."

"Hi, handsome." The voice on the other end of the line was melodious, but it failed to fill the emptiness around him.

There was only one woman who called him that. Tracey Harper, a woman who occasionally traveled in the same circles as he did. "Hello, Tracey."

The chuckle was deep and seductive. She'd perfected it, he thought absently. "Right the first time, handsome. I'm flattered. All those women around you and you still recognize my voice."

She was fishing for a compliment. He obliged. "I'd never forget your voice, Tracey. You've always been in a class all by yourself."

"Liar." She laughed, delighted. "But I must admit, I do like hearing your lies. You always do it so well. So tell me, where have you been hiding yourself?" she wanted to know.

"Nowhere. I've been working." Tracey's grandfather had made the family fortune and had been the last in his family actually to work. To Tracey, work was something to do if nothing more interesting and diverting came along. So far, she hadn't worked a day in her life.

"Now you really are lying," she said, her voice pouty. "I stopped by the firm on Tuesday to take you out to lunch and they said you were on vacation. But then Lyle Burnett swore he saw you downtown the other day. Lyle has excellent vision," she empha-sized. "What's going on, handsome? Have you thrown over your friends for a walk on the wild side?"

Funny, he'd never really noticed how completely shallow Tracey was until just now. He'd come across fingerprints that had more depth. "I'm doing a little work for Advocate Aid."

He heard her laugh on the other end, as if he'd just said something hopelessly amusing. "Community service, darling? Did the police pinch you for going too fast in that gorgeous car of yours?"

"No, no community service." He had no idea where this feeling of protectiveness toward the agen-cy had suddenly come from. It didn't really make sense. It wasn't as if he cared about the people he was dealing with, he just wanted to be done with it. So why— He decided it had to be Tracey's haughty attitude that was rubbing him the wrong way. "This is a favor to Jenny."

"Jenny?" she echoed as if the name meant nothing

to her. "Oh, right, Jennifer. Jenny. That sweet sister of yours." He could almost hear the smirk in her voice. "The one who never has any fun."

Jordan could feel his temper spiking. Exercising control, he managed to bank it down. Tracey Harper was too self-centered to realize she was being insulting and condescending. To Tracey, the world had been created solely for the purpose of serving as her playground.

"That's the one," he replied mildly. "Jenny's expecting a baby."

"Really?" Amusement fairly dripped from the word. Tracey had once declared she had no good use for children, as if their function was to be strictly utilitarian.

He went on with his explanation, looking for a way to end the conversation. This wasn't diverting, it was irritating. If anything, it made him think of Sarajane, and how worthless Tracey seemed in comparison to her.

"Her doctor ordered complete bed rest for her, so I'm filling in until she can find someone else to take her place." Maybe if she was bored with the conversation, Tracey would hang up, he thought. He didn't realize that he'd given her a cue until she responded.

"Hmm, speaking of beds, I just bought this sinfully expensive one last week. Had it custom made, actually. It's a huge circular bed." She paused as if waiting for the words to sink in and create an image. "I was wondering if you'd be interested in breaking it in with me, so to speak."

She was making, Jordan knew, an offer she felt he couldn't refuse. Tracey was one of those women who Michelangelo would have gone to the ends of the earth in pursuit of, hoping to use her as a model. She had what had once been described by a fashion magazine as "the perfect body."

Having seen it up close and personal, he could attest that if anything, the label was a modest one. And obviously from the conversation, for whatever reason, it was a body that, at least for tonight, she was very willing to share with him. He knew she probably felt that he should feel honored. But the thought of making love with Tracey until dawn between long, languid sips of champagne, didn't have the appeal for him that it had once had.

Tracey's body might have been perfect, but she had the morals of an alley cat and right now, he had neither the will nor the desire to cope with that. Try as he might, his thoughts were elsewhere.

He tried to let her down diplomatically. "I appreciate the offer, Tracey—"

She was way ahead of him. "But you pass," she guessed.

He backed up his decision with a reason, thinking to spare her pride. He doubted if anyone had ever turned down her offer before. "I've got this court case to prepare for."

"But handsome, not that I don't believe in free will and the justice system and all that tedious garbage, but this is Friday night. Court doesn't come around until Monday morning—does it?"

She probably didn't know for certain, he thought. Things like that didn't enter into her world. There were family lawyers for that. "No."

Her tone indicted that she'd made her case. "Well, that's eons away."

Not that he was worried, but Monday morning was closer than it appeared. "I never like walking into anything unprepared."

"That you don't," she agreed with a throaty chuckle. "For an untamed beast, you are the most prepared man I have ever had." She sighed, accepting his decision. He had no idea if she was disappointed or even cared that he wouldn't be part of her night. Someone else would and that was all she was interested in. "Well, if you change your mind, you know where to find me."

"I know where to find you," he assured her. Under *L* for *lost*, he thought.

Jordan broke the connection before Tracey could say anything further.

He looked at the phone for a moment. He supposed that was a stupid move on his part. Tracey Harper was ready, willing and able. Every man's dream. She would have been a perfect substitute for Sarajane.

He turned the key in the ignition, frowning.

No, that wasn't right. Tracey would have *never* been a substitute for Sarajane. The two women were worlds apart. Sarajane had more than a body—she had a mind, and a soul.

Sarajane, he mused, pulling away from the curb, whether she knew it or not, was the most complete woman he'd ever met.

Chapter Ten

Jordan saw the inside of the county jail not once, but three times over the course of the next two days, bringing Joe a new set of questions each time and burrowing himself, as much as possible, into the events of the man's life leading up to his arrest.

He did everything but engage in a course of presti-digitation to pull together a defense. If the case he had taken over from the public defender could be compared to a chicken, there wouldn't have even been enough meat available on the frame to make chicken soup. Five minutes into reading the notes it was obvious to Jordan that the attorney handling Joe Juarez's defense had considered this case a waste of his valuable time.

There was next to nothing in the file, no compilation of people who'd been interviewed or were waiting to be interviewed. There wasn't even a character witness slated to take the stand for the accused other than Joe's sister, Alicia.

He contrasted that dearth of people with Assistant District Attorney Janie French's list. The latter contained both of Joe's former employers and the engineer who had worked with him on the missing engine plans. It also cited several of the racers and the people who were part of the pit crew. Since the assistant district attorney was calling on them, that couldn't be good for their side, Jordan reasoned.

The first thing he did Monday morning was to go down to the courthouse to try to get a postponement. The effort went down in flames. The presiding judge wouldn't hear of it. Justice, like punishment, he maintained, should be meted out swiftly.

When Jordan drove down to Advocate Aid, he was not in the best of moods. His mood wasn't helped any when Sarajane all but jumped on him the moment he walked into the office.

"Where were you?" she demanded. All morning, she'd been anticipating seeing him walk through the door. This on the heels of a weekend that was equal parts longing and annoyance, both of which had their roots in their last encounter before her building. She'd thought of nothing else but him. And then when he hadn't shown up to work this morning, she'd had a sinking feeling he was using that "almost" incident not to come in any more.

She gestured toward the cheap clock on the back wall. "It's almost ten-thirty. The agreement was for you to show up for three weeks, not one."

He didn't need this. He was still trying to hang on to his temper from his encounter with the judge. She was in the direct line of fire and if she wasn't careful, he would give her both barrels. "I am aware of the terms of the agreement, Sarajane. And for your information, I was in court."

"Pleading or being arraigned?" she shot back, angry not because he was late, but because she cared that he was late. And nowhere in that small scenario did the people who were waiting to see him figure in. What was the matter with her? One stupid kiss, one almost-encounter, and she was forgetting what she was all about? "And what were you doing in court, anyway?" she wanted to know. "One of your old cases come up for air?"

"No," he countered tersely. He was not in the mood to be cornered and interrogated, especially not when it was being played out on a mini stage before strangers who made no effort to look as if they weren't listening. "One of yours. I was trying to get Joe Juarez's case postponed."

She immediately jumped to what she felt was the logical conclusion. "Why, don't you want to handle it?"

"You know—" he leaned in, his voice steely "—for

a woman who's busy dispensing hope and optimism to the masses, you certainly have a negative way of looking at things."

"You bring that out in me," she answered without missing a beat. And then, curiosity got the better of her. "Why were you trying to get it postponed?"

Failure of any kind did not sit well with him. He wasn't used to it and he didn't like it, even when it was only the small matter of getting a judge to privately rule in his favor in his chambers.

He also didn't care for explaining himself, but she was obviously like a dog with a bone. She wasn't about to let go until he told her everything.

"So that I could spend more time working up some sort of defense." He held up the file he'd taken with him on Friday. The one that had almost no pages inside of it. "This thing is anemic."

Sarajane caught her lower lip between her teeth. She couldn't exactly fault him for not being here if he was away doing a good thing. Damn him. "So when is the new trial date?"

His expression was positively black as he answered. "Tomorrow."

She looked at him, confused. "That's the old trial date."

"Yeah, I know." There was a touch of bitterness in his voice. Was he actually getting involved in these cases? With these people? She was still rather skeptical. People from his side of the silver spoon rarely leaped over to hers. "The judge wouldn't grant the postponement."

That didn't make any sense to her. "Why? According to Jenny, you have judges eating out of your hand all the time."

He laughed dryly, but there was no humor in the sound. "This one's liable to *eat* my hand. The Honorable Judge Karl Rhinehardt thinks that people should get the death penalty for jaywalking. And don't get him started on littering."

She stifled a shiver, thinking of what that would mean to Joe. "Can't we get another judge?"

Jordan shook his head. "Doesn't work that way. The only way to get another judge is either to have the judge recuse him- or herself, or find a reason to make them step down, such as citing something in their past that would show a prejudicial connection to the case. Being an ornery son of a bitch doesn't count."

That didn't sound very heartening. "So what do we do?"

He shrugged, draping his coat over the back of his chair. He noticed one of the people waiting eyeing the apparel. He was too annoyed to worry about someone making off with his coat. "Go in with guns blazing and use what we have."

She picked up on his tone. It was missing its positive verve. "Is that enough?"

No, he thought. But it did no good to talk about that. "It's going to have to be." At least there was one positive note. "I called in a favor and asked Rusty to nose around."

She cocked her head. The name meant nothing to her. "Rusty?"

Jordan realized that she wasn't familiar with his life, didn't know the people he dealt with in the firm, and why should she? They would have lived out their entire lives, their spheres never touching, if it hadn't been for Jenny.

"Rusty O'Hara," he told her. "He's Morrison and Treherne's private investigator."

Theirs, but not Advocate Aid's, she thought. "You can do that?"

It was a technicality. "Rusty's doing it after hours. Maybe he can help fill in the blanks." At least he hoped so.

"Blanks? There're blanks?" She wanted to ask what kind, but waited for him to tell her.

"I'm hoping there are. Otherwise, the way things look right now, your boy's guilty."

Feeling vulnerable and hating it, she didn't like what she thought he was implying. "He's not my boy, he's my friend's brother."

Jordan shrugged. "Figure of speech." He glanced over to the people lined up along the far wall, some seated, some standing, all waiting. Harry and Sheldon, who'd finally returned from his family emergency, were juggling the case load. Slowly. "Have I got time for coffee?"

Her impulse was to say *no*—that if he really wanted coffee, she would bring it to him; that he needed to get started. But he was late because he'd been working on Joe's case and she had to give him points for that.

So she nodded. "Sure. If it'll help get you on track."

He blew out a breath as he went to the supply room. It was going to take more than coffee, in this case lethal and black, to kill the frustration he was dealing with. "What'll help get me on track is something to sink my teeth into."

She hesitated for a second. "You mean food? We probably have—"

"No, I mean something to sink my teeth into regarding the case." Picking up the mug he distinctly remembered leaving on his desk but that had somehow found its way in here, he brought it over to the coffeemaker. Steam floated up to him as he poured. "Right now, everything points to Joe having taken the plans and the engine."

She didn't care about the obvious. She believed in Alicia who believed in Joe. It was as simple as that.

"But nobody found anything," she insisted. "The police couldn't find the missing engine or the plans—because Joe doesn't have them."

Jordan shook his head. "All that means is that Joe found somewhere safe to hide them until he rode this thing out."

"Or that someone else did," she countered with

feeling. "But the police wouldn't know that because they stopped looking when Joe's boss's son pointed a finger at him."

She caught his attention. Mug in hand, he leaned his back against the counter and took a sip. The tip of his tongue got burned, but he ignored it. "Why would he do that?" he wanted to know. "Is there bad blood between them?"

Sarajane nodded. "Alicia told me that Joe put Matt Lawrence in his place after he tried to rough up some girl at a local bar. Things got ugly and Joe had to defend himself."

"Do we know this woman's name?" The altercation would point to motive, he thought. Maybe the son was trying to get back at Joe by framing him. But he needed details, confirmation of the incident.

Sarajane shook her head.

Jordan stared down at the top of his mug, watching the way the overhead light danced along the black liquid. By his count, this was his fifth cup today. He still felt tired. That's what he got for putting in long hours at home, trying to find an angle to work on a case with only one angle—the one incriminating his client.

He thought about the report he'd gotten forwarded to his computer. More favors being called in. Who would have ever thought he'd be using up his supply on a case that would ultimately yield nothing more than a sense of satisfaction.

"You know," he began slowly, "Joe's not quite the knight in shining armor that you make him out to be."

Sarajane didn't like the sound of that. "Meaning what?"

"Meaning he ran with a gang when he was younger."

She breathed a sigh of relief. She was aware of that story. "Alicia said that was so he could survive in the neighborhood. But all that's behind him."

"Maybe so, but he was still arrested for joyriding in a stolen vehicle."

Alicia had made it a point to tell her everything about her brother so that there would be no surprises. "He was fourteen and he didn't know it was stolen."

"I'm not the one you have to convince," he reminded her. "These are all things the A.D.A. will parade around before the jury, most likely on the first day." His frustration level flared again. "Hell, there's not enough to drag the case out to the end of the week if we don't come up with something and soon."

She looked at him pointedly. "So, come up with something. You're the famous lawyer who's never lost a case, remember?"

He was surprised that she knew that. And that the information was followed up with a wisecrack. He didn't bother asking her where she got her information. Suffice to say that it was true.

And that it was in jeopardy of becoming history. *His* history.

"I'm doing my best, Sarajane," he told her as he began to head back into the communal room. "I'm doing my best."

Jordan felt numb.

More than that, he felt frustrated.

Numb because it looked as if his winning streak was about to come to an abrupt and untimely end. And frustrated because it really didn't have to be that way if only he had a little more time to do his job.

But Judge Rhinehardt refused even to entertain his request for a recess, much less any of his objections to the things that the assistant district attorney was saying. The latter's statements were clearly prejudicial from where Jordan was sitting. He could see the jury drifting away from his client, taken for that ride by cleverly worded innuendoes.

Rhinehardt overruled every one of his objections.

Sarajane was growing more agitated by the moment. Since Alicia was to be a character witness, she wasn't allowed to be in the courtroom for the rest of the proceedings, so Sarajane served as Joe Juarez's only cheering section.

Sitting in the first row behind the defendant's table, she leaned forward and urgently whispered, "Can't you do something?" to Jordan. "That witch is driving nails into Joe's coffin." The "witch" she was referring to was the A.D.A.

Jordan glanced at Sarajane. It was on the tip of his tongue to ask her what she'd have him do since every objection he'd posed so far had been summarily over-ruled. And then it came to him.

Jordan suddenly rose to his feet and cried, "I object."

Rhinehardt, his broad features partially hidden behind the white whiskers he'd been sporting for the last ten years, looked momentarily confused. He stopped his gavel from making contact in midswing. "To what, Mr. Hall? The assistant district attorney hasn't said anything."

Jordan drew himself up to his full six feet. He'd never been afraid to speak his mind. He hadn't been raised to back down out of fear or concern that speaking might hurt his career. Standing his ground, he looked Rhinehardt squarely in the eyes.

"I object to this whole process. And to you, Your Honor."

Taken aback, Rhinehardt recovered almost instantly. He banged his gavel loudly, his eyes narrowing into dark slits.

"Take care, Mr. Hall, I am only cutting you a little leeway because of your father. But know that you are skating on very thin ice right now."

Sarajane fully expected Jordan to apologize and sit down. She couldn't believe it when he remained standing, like a warrior determined to fight to the death.

"Better than being thin-skinned. Or pea-brained," Jordan added, his inference clear.

The face beneath the white whiskers was turning red. "You, sir, are in contempt."

Jordan took the judge's statement and ran with it. Coming around the defense table, he began to walk toward the judge without asking for the customary permission to approach.

"You bet I am," Jordan declared. "I'm in contempt of you and this entire sham of a proceeding. You're so blinded by what you deem to be your own light, that you're refusing to listen to reason."

The judge blustered. No one else in the courtroom spoke. To Sarajane, it sounded like no one else was even breathing. She certainly wasn't. "One more word, and I'm sending you to jail."

"Just one more word?" Jordan asked, feigning surprise. "How about a lot more words, Judge?" He was at the judge's bench now, looking up at the man. "All of them about you. And none of them flattering."

Jordan had to raise his voice in order to have the last part of his sentence heard. Rhinehardt was banging down his gavel and the sound triggered a response in kind from the people in the courtroom. Suddenly, everyone was talking at once.

The judge's voice rose above the rest. "I am fining you two thousand dollars. Mr. Hall! Say one more word and it'll be three." He twisted around in his seat, scanning the courtroom for help. "Bailiff, take Mr. Hall to the holding cell!" he roared.

Sarajane watched, horrified, as two large, official-looking men with guns strapped to their sides appeared to flank Jordan. Between them, they escorted the attorney from the courtroom, leaving behind a very befuddled looking Joe in their wake.

"What the hell was all that about?"

Jordan looked up from the seat he'd taken in the prison cell. Sarajane was standing on the other side of the bars. She had her hands wrapped around them, looking at him intently.

Jordan noted several of the men in the cell with him, brought there by a variety of charges, were all united in the way they were leering at Sarajane. He rose, crossing over to her, attempting to block her body from view with his own. He could do at least that much for her, he reasoned.

"Venting my anger," he answered her. "And, more importantly, buying Joe some valuable time."

She caught on immediately and looked at him, stunned. "You mean to tell me that all that was just to get the trial postponed until tomorrow?" which was when the judge had announced that they would reconvene.

"Not all," Jordan admitted, then added, "but most."

He would have never given in to the anger on his own, but he wasn't in this for himself, he was trying to get Joe acquitted. Getting himself thrown into jail brought the trial to a grinding halt since he was Joe's only attorney on record and every man was still entitled to representation before a judge.

She looked at him with new respect. "Jordan, I'm impressed. You're devious."

He laughed shortly. "I'm a lawyer," he reminded her. "Devious goes with the territory. Listen—" he shifted slightly, sensing that one of the men was doing his damnedest to get a better look at her "—I appreciate you stopping by, but I should be out by morning, so why don't you go—"

"You'll be out now," she contradicted him, turning toward the entrance. A bailiff was approaching with the keys. He unlocked the door.

Jordan looked at Sarajane. "What's this?"

"The smell of freedom, Jordan," she answered flippantly. "You're free to go. Your fine's been paid."

Jordan picked up his jacket from the seat where he'd left it and quickly vacated the cell. "Advocate Aid has that kind of money?" He wanted to know as he slipped the jacket back on.

Wouldn't that be lovely? Sarajane thought. So much more could be done if they had more funding. She shook her head. "No."

They walked through the door, leaving the cells behind. "Then how—"

Eric was waiting for them on the other side of the door. Leaning against the wall, he straightened now and grinned at his brother-in-law.

"She called me. Or rather, she called Jenny. Who, if she wasn't bedridden right now, would have been knocked for a loop and on the floor." Eric looked at him as if he had never seen him before. "Just exactly when did this little epiphany of yours strike?" he wanted to know.

"No epiphany," Jordan informed him. He took a breath. Freedom definitely had better air, he thought. "It was just that, with the way Rhinehardt seemed bent on railroading Joe Juarez, it seemed like the only way I could buy him a little extra time. I wouldn't be surprised to find out that he's being used as a scapegoat."

"Then you do believe him." Sarajane's tone told him that she was relieved and happy about this turn of events.

"It's not a question of believing him, it's a question of getting him the defense he's entitled to. But yes, if it makes a difference to you, I believe him. But whether I do or not isn't what's going to get him off."

"You also didn't manage to buy him much time," Eric pointed out as they walked out of the building and down the stone steps to the parking lot. "Court's reconvening tomorrow morning."

Something was better than nothing, Jordan thought. "That only gives Rusty tonight to see what he can find out, maybe get a bead on that kid Joe got into a fight with. Since we're dealing with circumstantial evidence, we need to find out who really took the plans."

"Can Rusty do that in such a short amount of time?" Eric wanted to know.

Jordan shook his head. "I have no idea." He could only cross his fingers and pray.

"Well, I've got an office to get back to." Eric clapped him on the back. "You might give Jenny a call later, tell her you survived the Big House, let her gush a little over you. She thinks you've come over to her way of thinking. Me, I need more convincing." He laughed, shaking his head before walking off to his car. "My brother-in-law, the jailbird."

"*Crusader's* more like it." It wasn't until the two men turned to look at her that Sarajane realized she'd said the words out loud.

Chapter Eleven

Eric laughed louder. "Now there's a word you don't often hear applied to you." He smiled at Sarajane. "You obviously need more experience with crusaders, Sarajane." His eyes shifted to his friend. "See you around, Jordy. Stay out of trouble."

And with that, Eric left the two of them in the parking lot.

Sarajane's complexion had turned that intriguing shade of pink again. "Don't mind him. I liked being called a crusader."

She was sure he did. Damn, why couldn't the earth open up and swallow her? Then she wouldn't have to stand here, desperately trying to regain lost ground. "I tend to say the first thing that comes to mind when I'm caught off guard."

Reaching his vehicle, he opened the passenger door for her. "What caught you off guard?"

"You," she answered honestly, getting in. "I didn't expect you to go the extra mile for someone who can't pay that exorbitant fee of yours."

He got in on his side and started up his car. It was nice to be out of that metal enclosure. He suddenly felt an overwhelming wave of sympathy for Joe Juarez. "Why is it even when you give me a compliment, it sounds like a criticism?"

She shrugged, sitting back in her seat, looking straight ahead. Avoiding his face. It was easier that way. "Maybe it's because you're too good-looking."

"What?" That made absolutely no sense to him.

She spared him a quick glance. "Good-looking men tend to be shallow."

This again. He'd always hated generalities, those broad, sweeping statements that mindlessly wiped out an entire population with their thoughtless rhetoric. But this was Sarajane and she had gotten him out, so he was willing to be tolerant. And maybe even a little amused because she looked so serious.

"And I take it you've conducted an intensive study on this?"

He saw her stiffen in her seat, as if under physical attack. "I've had experience."

What, one boyfriend who turned out to be a rat?

Two? He doubted if there'd been more men in her life than that. For one thing, she was too young, for another, she seemed to be entirely caught up in her work. First one there, last one gone. As far as he could see, that left her very little time for socializing.

"Okay, I'll bite," he said gamely. "How much experience have you had?"

She avoided looking at him. "Enough."

That's what he thought. Jordan eased his foot off the gas onto the brake as the light up ahead turned red. "You're how old?"

Sarajane bristled. "What does my age have to do with it?"

As a lawyer, he knew evasion when he heard it. "I'd take your declaration a little more seriously if you were approaching fifty. At less than half that, you haven't been around enough men to form even a preliminary opinion."

Typical male thinking. Sarajane raised her chin defensively. "I *have* been around enough."

He wasn't about to leave that unexplored, even if he didn't find himself becoming progressively more interested in her, which he was. By the second. He even felt a smattering of jealousy stirring.

"How many were 'enough'?" He watched her press her lips together. From out of nowhere he felt a longing to have those same lips repeat the action against his. "C'mon, Sarajane, if I'm to give your theory any credence at all, I need an answer."

Her eyes narrowed stubbornly, as she braced herself for ridicule. "Two."

"Two," he echoed incredulously.

The light had turned to green. Since he wasn't moving, she gestured him on. "Two."

"Two," he repeated for a second time, shaking his head. Foot on the gas, he began driving again. "You do realize, don't you, that two's the lowest number, besides one, you could come up with." When she made no response, he added, "I thought you were supposed to be so open-minded."

She scowled at him. How did this become about her? She'd just rescued his sorry hide out of jail, he was supposed to be grateful, not combative.

"Shouldn't you be preparing for tomorrow?" she asked him in an icy tone.

The laugh was short and dismissive. With no clues, no leads and, troublingly, a suddenly uncooperative accused, the matter was temporarily out of his hands. "At this point, if Rusty doesn't come up with something, the only way I can prepare for this case is to find the nearest church and start lighting candles. Joe Juarez did a one-eighty on us. He now wants me to back off and let him get sent away for the crime."

When had this happened? The last she'd heard, Joe was claiming to be innocent. Jordan had to have gotten it wrong. "That's ridiculous."

"I went to see him three times this weekend to try

to build some kind of a case for him." Juarez was a completely different man from the one he'd first interviewed when he accepted the case on Friday. "The first two times, he was all gung-ho. The last visit, I got the impression that he was giving up. Not because he was hopeless, but just because. Something, or someone, changed his mind."

Sarajane refused to believe him. "You're imagining things."

"I wish I were." Having nothing but circumstantial evidence was difficult enough, but without the accused cooperating, they might as well call it a day and wait for the judge's sentence.

Sarajane looked at him, mystified. "Why would a man willingly go to prison?"

Jordan had been asking himself that same question since Saturday. "My best guess is either he's guilty and is suffering from one hell of a bout of remorse—"

She waited for him to follow it up. When he didn't, she prodded, "Or?"

This alternative, to him, seemed to be the more likely of the two scenarios. During the last visit with Joe on the weekend, he'd seemed distracted, as if he were worried about something. "Or he's protecting someone and this case is bigger than it looks."

As far as she knew, from what Alicia had told her, Joe wasn't seeing anyone. His whole world was work and his kids. "Who would he be protecting?"

Again, Jordan laughed dryly under his breath. "If I had the answer to that, tomorrow would be a slam dunk for our side."

It wasn't.

As it turned out, with Judge Rhinehardt all but visibly hostile toward the defense and Joe Juarez unable or unwilling to come up with anything that would cause at least some members of the jury to be inclined to have doubts about his guilt, by the day's end, Jordan saw his perfect, spotless record for winning cases go down in flames.

The jury returned to the courtroom after spending barely twenty minutes deliberating. The verdict was *guilty.*

In the sum total of things, the loss was hardly noticeable.

But he noticed. For him, it stood out in ten-foot-high, glaring letters.

You lost.

There was nothing Jordan hated more than losing. Especially when he felt he was in the right. Closed mouth or not, there was something about his client that bespoke innocence.

He'd tried one last time this morning to make Joe come around just before the judge made his entrance into the courtroom.

Leaning to his left, he'd kept his voice low. "C'mon, Joe, there's got to be something you can give me, something I can work with in order to keep you out of prison."

But Joe was stoic. From his expression, he appeared to have made his peace with what was to be. "You're wasting your time, counselor. Thanks for the effort, but just leave this alone. You've done your best."

He hadn't done anything at all, yet, Jordan thought, except get frustrated. He lowered his voice even more, whispering the words into Joe's ear. "If you feel guilty for some reason, think of your kids. They need a father around."

Joe drew his head back enough to look Jordan in the eye. He looked determined. "I *am* thinking of the kids. I'm doing this for them."

Jordan felt a sliver of temper surge. "What the hell is that supposed to mean?"

Joe shook his head, folding his hands before him as if he were in school. Just like Alicia, Jordan couldn't help thinking. "I can't say anything further." Those were his last words on the subject.

"I'm your lawyer, you can tell me anything and it won't go any further until you give me permission." He *needed* to know what was going on.

But Joe looked determined to keep his own counsel and then the judge entered the courtroom. A hush fell over the crowd just before they all rose.

It was downhill after that.

* * *

"We'll appeal," Jordan promised Joe with feeling as he saw the bailiff approaching.

"It's okay." Joe's expression belonged to a man resigned to his fate. "Don't bother. I got what I deserved."

Gene Russo, the older of the two owners of the racing team pushed through the crowd and reached the defense table before anyone could stop him. Broad and over six feet tall, he looked particularly menacing when angry. And he was angry.

"Where's the hell's the damn engine, you miserable bastard?" he demanded. Two more bailiffs came running over to intervene before the scene could get out of hand, each grabbing Russo by the arm.

Joe looked at his former boss, oddly calm in the face of this abrupt threat. "I'm sorry," he said just before cuffs were snapped on his wrists.

Russo was dragged away in the opposite direction, his path marked by a barrage of curses.

"He looked relieved to be found guilty," Sarajane said, stunned, as she came around to join Jordan.

Jordan was packing up his briefcase, strictly on automatic pilot. He didn't like what had happened here today. None of it. "Looked that way, didn't it?"

Sarajane craned her neck, watching as the bailiff took Joe out of the courtroom. A distraught Alicia had left moments after the verdict, hurrying out to the niece and nephew she was caring for.

It didn't make sense to her, Sarajane thought, looking toward Jordan for enlightenment. "Why?"

Beat the hell out of him, Jordan thought. He snapped the locks shut. "That is the sixty-four-thousand-dollar question."

Sarajane thought that an odd sum of money to cite. "What?"

It was in reference to one of the first classic game shows in the fifties. "Way before your time," he commented. He picked up his briefcase and began to head toward the exit. "Before mine, too," he added with an ironic smile. He held the door open for her. "Juarez is my first loss."

She was acutely aware of that. In an odd way, she felt responsible, because if she hadn't egged Jordan on, maybe he would have handed the case off to one of the other attorneys. But she had wanted Joe to have the best. And the best had lost. In a circular way, that made breaking his record her fault.

"C'mon," she coaxed once they were outside in the parking lot, "I'll buy you dinner." It was precious small consolation, but it was the best she could do.

Jordan tossed his briefcase into the backseat of his car. "Don't feel much like eating tonight. I need a drink."

"Okay," she agreed gamely. "I'll buy you that instead." Jordan looked at her in mild bemusement. "Don't look so surprised. I drink," she informed him. "On occasion."

He got in behind the wheel and turned on the ignition. "Well, if ever there was an occasion to drink, this is it."

They got the last spot in the parking lot. Mother's Bar and Grill was located several blocks away from the courthouse. It was more bar than grill and Mother was actually "Dutchman" Van Damme, a former hockey-player-slash-reborn-biker with jet-black hair on his knuckles, three missing teeth and a physique that stopped anyone short of King Kong from giving him any flack.

Despite appearances, Dutchman had a pleasant enough manner and the drinks he placed before Jordan and Sarajane were not watered down. Their problem however, was that they went down much too smoothly.

After the fourth round, Sarajane lost count. The ache in her chest, however, was much harder to lose. The more she consumed, the worse she felt for Alicia, for Joe. And for Jordan.

She shifted on her barstool, finding it more and more difficult to maintain her perch.

"This really shouldn't count, you know. As a loss," she added when Jordan looked at her quizzically. Her fingers were wrapped tightly around her glass and as she spoke, she was inclined to gesture. A tiny wave of alcohol punctuated her last statement, splashing down onto the bar after dribbling along her knuckles.

Maybe it was the alcohol, but he didn't follow her reasoning. "Why shouldn't it count?"

She took a deep breath and looked at him patiently, as if he was being simple-minded. "Because you didn't have any time to get into the case. It was sprung on you, I mean, it was spranged—" Sarajane stopped, listening to the word she'd just said echo in her head. "Is that a word?"

He smiled. From where she sat, his lips blended in with the glass. The blue neon light from behind the bar was casting eerie beams along his face. "I'm pretty sure it's not."

"Oh." She cocked her head, thinking. Replaying the word again. "Sounds like a word," she decided. "If it wasn't a word, could I say it?"

He laughed. The lady, he thought, was quite drunk. And rather adorable at that. "Good question."

She nodded. "Yup, it is." She paused to take another sip of her quickly evaporating drink. "I'm full of good questions. Want to hear another one?"

Amused, he turned the stool to face her better. "Shoot."

Sarajane opened her mouth, then closed it again, a puzzled expression on her face. *She was going to have one hell of a hangover tomorrow,* he thought. The one waiting for him wasn't going to be small potatoes, either. He'd gone past a buzz forty-five minutes ago, but apparently he had a better capacity for holding his liquor than she did.

"Okay, ask."

"Oh, right." Sarajane closed her eyes for a second. Ordinarily, it helped her focus. Right now, it just caused the darkened room to start spinning. As it began to pick up speed at an alarming rate, creating havoc in her stomach, her eyes flew open. She found herself looking right up at him. "Why do I want to make love with you when you're bad for me?"

The question, uttered without any warning, sobered him a good deal. And then he smiled at her. He sincerely doubted she'd remember any of this in the morning. For her sake, he hoped she wouldn't. Otherwise, she would turn a permanent shade of red. "The same reason a moth flies into a flame, I'd imagine."

As she pondered the meaning of that, she saw the bartender approaching. Her focus shifted immediately. So much so that she almost slid off the stool. Jordan managed to anchor her down at the last moment. She never even noticed.

"Oh good, you're here. One more, please." She pushed her empty glass toward the Dutchman.

He made no move to take it or to fill it. Instead, he shook his head the way an indulgent parent might at a favorite child. "You've had enough tonight, honey. I'm cutting you off."

She drew herself up indignantly. "You can't do that," she informed him, then looked at Jordan a tad sheepishly. "Can he do that?"

"He can do that," Jordan assured her.

"Oh." She looked thoughtful for a moment. "Then I guess we'd better go somewhere else to get our liquid libation," she slurred.

The bartender looked at both of them skeptically. "You want me to call you a cab?" he asked Jordan.

Sarajane giggled, then covered her mouth to stop the sound. "He's not a cab, he's Jordan. A first-rate lawyer. Except that he lost today. His first time." She shook her head and look genuinely downcast as she added, "My fault. All my fault."

Jordan saw the bartender reach under the bar and place a portable phone on the counter. He began to dial. Jordan shook his head, momentarily stopping him.

"I'll take her home," he assured the burly man in his best courtroom argument voice.

The phone remained where it was and the bartender began dialing again. "You're not driving from my place," he informed Jordan. There was no arguing with his no-nonsense tone. "I've been through that once. Let a guy go who was three sheets to the wind. Got my butt sued off." It was clear he'd been about to use a different word to describe the part that had suffered, then had decided to clean it up because of the mixed company. "Ain't looking to have that happen again."

Cocking her head again, Sarajane leaned over the counter, holding on to steady herself as she took a look at the bartender's hind quarters. "It grew back," she announced in case he didn't know.

"We'll walk it off," he promised the bartender. "Her place isn't too far from here."

It was obvious that the bartender was skeptical about the outcome. "A block is a long way to go when you're in her condition."

Jordan was already slipping Sarajane's coat up her arms, onto her shoulders. "Don't worry, I'll take good care of her."

The bartender looked somewhat uncertain as he regarded Sarajane. "You all right with that? His taking you home?"

Terrific, Jordan thought. *She's got a knight in dented armor looking out for her.*

"I'm great with that," she answered the man. "Jordan's as honorable as they come."

Jordan was struggling to get the coat back on Sarajane, who kept shrugging it off the moment he had it on her shoulders. "C'mon, Sarajane," he coaxed.

"I'm hot," Sarajane declared, trying to shrug off the coat again.

This time, he held it in place with his palms against her upper arms. "Yes you are, but that's beside the point. I need to get you home."

His words evoked a response from her he wasn't prepared for, but then, things seemed to be going that route with her lately.

"You feel it, too?" she asked, wide-eyed as she turned around to face him. The brush of her body against his sent off a chain reaction in his.

"Feel what?" he asked evasively. He began to guide her toward the front door.

She half stumbled along, clinging to him for support and yet somehow blissfully unaware that she needed it. "That heat pulsing all through you."

"Whatever you say." Somehow, she'd managed to shrug off one side of her coat again. He caught the end and tugged it back up her arm. "Be a good girl and leave your arms in the sleeves."

She laughed, allowing him to dress her. "I'd rather put my arms around you."

"Later," he told her.

She took a deep breath to steady herself as they made it through the bar's front door. "When later?"

"Later, later."

"Oh. Okay," she responded cheerfully.

Feeling somewhat unsteady himself, it took Jordan a while to get her to her apartment even though it was only three blocks away. Sarajane barely weighed a hundred and ten pounds, and he was very grateful for that. It made it easy to maneuver her down the street. Arriving at her building, he carefully propelled her through the heavy front door and to the elevator. When it arrived, he propped her up against the railing to keep her from sinking to the floor.

Once they got to her floor, he got his arm beneath hers and tucked it around her torso. The two of them did a rather strange two-step to her door.

Still holding her up, Jordan instructed, "Give me your keys, Sarajane."

He expected an argument. Instead, she surprised him by digging into her coat pocket and handing the keys to him obediently. Sober or inebriated, the woman was nothing if not unpredictable.

When he opened the door, he saw that every light in the apartment was on. Jordan shook his head as he closed the door behind him.

"Wasteful," he commented.

"Missy was the last one out," Sarajane mumbled. "She forgets to turn them off."

There didn't seem to be any sign of the other woman around. "Where is she?" He didn't like the idea of leaving Sarajane alone in this condition.

"In San Francisco. Business," Sarajane added after a beat as the rest of her thought came to her. Then she grinned. "Or pleasure. I can't remember."

Jordan frowned. This wasn't good. "Then you're alone?"

"Nope." Before he knew it, Sarajane had thrown her arms around his neck and was leaning dangerously into him. There wasn't enough room for a sigh between their bodies. "You're here."

Chapter Twelve

Jordan took firm hold of her hands and began to unclasp Sarajane's arms from around his neck. Or attempted to.

The woman was obviously stronger than she looked, he thought. Pulling her arms away required more than the little bit of effort he was initially set to exert. It was like trying to pry apart two opposite ends of a horseshoe.

He was more tempted to remain than she could possibly ever know. "But I'm leaving," he told her.

Because if I don't go now, I'm not going to and we're both going to regret this in the morning, you more than me.

"Don't," she whispered, the single word feathering lightly along his face, along with her breath.

Jordan felt his gut tightening like a fist that was ready to swing. She'd left no room between them as she made her entreaty. No room for him even to draw in a safe breath.

He tried to step back. The look in her eyes pulled him in. The longing within his own body doubled. Again. "Sarajane, you don't know what you're asking."

"Yes, I do," she insisted softly. "I'm a big girl, Jordan. I know what happens between a man and a woman who are as attracted to each other as we are."

He wanted to deny it, to tell her she was just imagining the attraction. But for his part, it was there and he knew it. Was she telling him that she felt the same way? That he was on her mind as much as she was on his?

Or was that all just a by-product of four shots of amber liquid, served up too fast and consumed even faster? He didn't want to take any more chances than he already had.

"Sarajane, you've had too much to drink—" he began, once again making the effort to disentangle himself from her.

She allowed him to remove her arms from around his neck. But she held her ground, taking no step away. Her hands clasped behind her back, she moved in for the kill, using her body like a well-primed weapon to block his path. To brush up against his.

"Not too much," she told him confidently. "Just enough to let me do this."

Before Jordan had the chance to ask her what "this" was, Sarajane showed him. Momentarily framing his face with her hands, she brought her mouth up to his, successfully stopping any exchange of words that might have been forthcoming on his part.

Damn, but she tasted sweet.

Sweeter than anything he could remember having encountered. Ever.

So sweet that he immediately wanted more. And more after that. It was like falling headlong into a bottomless well.

Jordan allowed himself a moment, just a moment, in which to lose himself in her. To run his hands along her soft back, to deepen the kiss that stirred his soul. His tongue touched hers and he found it hopelessly erotic when she returned the favor.

For just a second, he pretended that this was something that was meant to be. That everything was all right and would continue to be that way.

For just a second, he lied to himself.

His heart was hammering wildly by the time his logical mind cried for a time-out. His sense of honor demanded it.

His body had never hated his code of ethics as much as it did now.

But he was bound by it, so he drew back, his hands on her shoulders as much to hold himself back as her in place. The look in her eyes wasn't making it easy for him. "Damn it, Sarajane, help me out here. I'm trying to do the right thing."

He watched in sheer fascination as her smile unfurled along her mouth. It was like being witness to the sunrise—if the sunrise were created out of sheer mischief.

"Seems to me you got it pretty right on the first pass, counselor." This time she did thread her arms back up around his neck. "But we can keep practicing if you like." Her smile pulled him farther in, making him almost weak. "I know I'd like."

Wicked. That was the word for it. She was positively wicked. Which seemed appropriate since she tasted of sin even though she smelled like heaven.

He continued to struggle to do the right thing. To keep from taking what was being offered because some higher plane demanded it. "I don't want to take advantage of you."

Her eyes were laughing at him and yet he couldn't take offense. "In case you haven't noticed, counselor, I'm the one taking advantage of you. You're just standing still. You will stand still for me, won't you?" she coaxed wantonly. "Otherwise, I can't do this."

And there were her lips again, pressed against his. Making him want her in ways he knew he shouldn't. He felt the last shreds of possible victory slipping away from him. Jordan held her against him, his body already hard from the desire that was racing through him with an urgency he found difficult to keep at bay.

He placed himself at her mercy. "I'm only so strong, Sarajane. I can't keep pushing you away."

"Then don't," she coaxed. "Don't push." She smiled and he could feel the effects of that smile penetrating all facets of him, going deep into his bones. What the hell was going on here? He hadn't had that much to drink, and yet, he felt drunk, completely and utterly drunk. "It'll go a lot easier on you," she promised.

Her eyes were still laughing at him and somehow, that made him want her all the more.

"Damn it," he swore under his breath, "I can't keep fighting both of us."

"Good."

She sealed her mouth back to his. And the rest of his willpower was melted away in the heat she generated within his very core.

Jordan surrendered.

He gave up all attempts to try to be noble. Gave up trying to hold himself in check and her at something close to arm's length. This had become more of a losing battle than the one he had faced at court today.

My oh my.

The old-fashioned phrase echoed in her brain over and over again as in the blink of an eye, she suddenly stopped being the hunter and found, deliciously, that she had turned into the hunted.

Yes!

The fire that had been progressively simmering in her veins ignited the moment Jordan touched her intimately, delving beneath the layers of her clothing, skimming along her flesh gently but with an urgency that all but made her swallow her own tongue.

Her first climax found her then.

Sarajane made no effort to restrain the moan that broke free as enjoyment, pure, raw and completely unadulterated, flashed through her with a speed that made lightening seem slow and labored.

She could tell her heavy breathing excited him, which in turn excited her.

He was exactly as she knew he would be, a fantastic lover, versed in ways that could make her body sing and her soul weep for joy.

And his mouth, oh, his wonderful mouth. She could have gone on kissing him all night. His lips made her feel more intoxicated than any of the tiny-umbrellaed drinks she'd consumed tonight. The more Jordan kissed her, the more her head felt as if it was spinning, until finally, she was literally clinging to him, afraid of letting go. Afraid of sinking to the floor because her knees had apparently gone on some exotic holiday, deserting her in her hour of need.

She didn't remember exactly when she began undressing him.

For the most part, Sarajane was entirely focused on what he was doing to her. Every one of his movements were embossed on her mind. Every place his lips, his teeth, his tongue touched seemed to dissolve and then reform into a mass of burning molten lava.

Breathing became more and more of a challenge as there was less and less air entering and leaving her body. Somehow, if her ears weren't playing tricks on her, she did manage to get him into a similar condition, but for the life of her, she didn't remember how.

Her mind kept winking in and out, caught between the outer stratosphere and what was happening right here in her apartment. Her bedroom, she amended, because they had managed to get there from the living room, although again, she didn't remember when or how, only that it had obviously happened, because here they were, on her bed, as naked as the day they had both been born.

His hands, firm, capable, confident, raced up and down her body, making her his as surely as if he'd held a branding iron in one of them and applied it.

His.

Damn, but she had sworn she'd never be in this position again. That if she were making love, it would be to someone who was diverting, entertaining, but not someone she could lose her heart to.

But that, it seemed, was the only way she could make love. By losing her heart. With her it was a case of the heart coming first and the rest of her following, not the other way around. It was, simply put, who and what she was. And right now, what Sarajane was was deliriously happy.

With effort, Sarajane struggled to keep from sinking into a hazy state of sheer contentment. Men did not respond to passive partners. Besides, what she was feeling was as far from passive as the earth was from the moon. So when Jordan kissed, she kissed, when he caressed, she caressed, making certain to make love to every part of him just as he was making love to every part of her.

Angles were taken, positions assumed and then surrendered. It was a workout worthy of a gold-medal-winning Olympic gymnast.

And when she finally lay beneath him and opened her legs to draw him in, Sarajane experienced the strangest feeling, not of illness brought on by drinking, not of exhaustion brought on by an almost superhuman amount of activity, but of peace amid the rising crescendo that was still beckoning to her. Peace, and an overwhelming sense of homecoming.

It had to do with the amount of alcohol she'd consumed, Sarajane silently insisted.

But even then she knew she was lying. Lying to preserve herself. Alcohol had nothing to do with this feeling.

And then, all thoughts but one vanished from her brain—the thought, the desire, to reach that one last pinnacle. With him, the man whose heart was drumming against her own. The man who had made her forget herself and her vows.

The momentum went on building until she thought she could hardly stand it. Her heart was pounding, her needs enormous. And then the eruption came, drenching her, encompassing him.

Her arms wrapped around him, Sarajane arched, pressing his body against hers, and prayed that time would find some way to freeze and stop completely. Because this was perfection. This fragile single moment in time had brought with it everything she had ever wanted or wished for.

But then her breathing returned to normal, bringing with it the surrounding area, drawing it back into focus. She became aware of where she was. Aware of the long, lanky man whose body was covering hers. Strange how she almost felt his weight, but didn't. How did he manage that?

When she felt him stirring, a bittersweet feeling washed over her. She didn't want reality returning, bringing the inevitable disappointment she knew was waiting for her with it. She wanted to lie here with him like this and pretend that every evening would be just like this. That every morning would find them together.

You're losing your mind, a tiny voice whispered. She ignored it. Being steeped in alcohol made it easier to do that.

Rising up on his elbows, feeling exhausted and entertaining a feeling of guilt that was growing at an alarming rate, Jordan looked down at her. He'd thought he had more self-control than that. What the hell was wrong with him?

He tried to frame an apology and felt the words sticking together, refusing to emerge coherently. "This wasn't supposed to happen."

A last sigh of contentment escaped as she looked up at him. As she absorbed the warmth from his body. "But it did."

"But it wasn't supposed to happen," he repeated with feeling. He wanted to say more, but, for once, his gift with words deserted him.

"We just went through this," she pointed out glibly.

It was her turn to raise herself up on her elbows. Her head did two complete rotations before she managed to pull it back into focus. His eyes were serious, she thought. He really meant what he was saying. Despite the way her head refused to settle down, something inside her felt a sharp sting of disappointment. Now that it was over, he wished he hadn't done it, she thought.

"Don't you think you should give it a little more time before you start dwelling on the regrets you're having?"

He read between the lines, or thought he did. "I don't regret making love with you. I regret the way you're going to feel about that in the morning. And that I'm going to be the source of *your* regrets."

She blinked, trying to understand what he had just said. Right now, only linear thoughts could get through. And then she laughed.

"You know, you more or less *had* to become a lawyer. Because you really don't make any sense as a regular person," she murmured.

Suddenly, she was sleepy. Very sleepy. So sleepy she couldn't keep her eyes open. Whatever else she was going to say to him vanished out of her head. The next moment, with her arm spread across his chest and her nude body curled up against his, she was sound asleep.

Jordan tried, for a moment, to ease away from her. To lift her arm and duck out from beneath it, only to find that he couldn't accomplish either. Somehow, she had managed to get a death grip on him and the only way he was going to get out from under it was literally to throw her off. Which took, he decided, much too much effort to accomplish without waking her.

So he remained where he was, telling himself it was only for a few minutes.

Just a few minutes.

The thought was still pulsating in his brain when he opened his eyes again. He thought he'd drifted off for only a little while.

Two seconds later he realized he'd slept away more than half the night. It was closer to morning than not. He had to leave.

Jordan knew he needed to slip out while Sarajane was still sleeping. He had absolutely no excuse available to him, nothing he could use to explain why he had done what he had. Blaming it on the moonlight, or the alcohol, or even on her seductive powers, didn't seem right somehow. He was a man, he was supposed to have more self-control than that.

The sad truth of it was, he didn't. Moreover, he hadn't wanted any. But that was a story for some other time.

Right now, he needed to get away.

But, as he raised her arm from its position on his chest—it seemed that she hadn't moved all night; from the looks of it, neither one of them had, content to remain in one another's shadow—Sarajane stirred. The next moment, she was opening her eyes.

And the very next moment after that, she bolted upright.

A little yelp of utter dismay escaped her lips as she yanked up what there was available of the sheet to cover herself. The pink color he was becoming so fond of spread like prairie fire over her cheeks.

Staring at him wide-eyed, Sarajane murmured numbly, "It wasn't a dream."

"No," he replied, assuming that she was referring to their night of lovemaking, his tone low, subdued, to keep her from thinking that he was gloating. "It wasn't." Looking at her face, feeling that same urgent pull inside beginning all over again, he couldn't resist feathering his fingers through her hair. "Even though it might have felt like one. At least it did on my end."

Her eyes fluttering shut, Sarajane put her hand to

her head. Half a dozen of the mine workers from *Snow White and the Seven Dwarfs* were pounding madly in her head with pickaxes. Any second now, they were going to break through.

She'd never had a hangover before.

"What happened?" she wanted to know.

Jordan proceeded with caution, beginning at the beginning. "We were trying to drown our sorrows over our loss in court."

She took a deep breath, hoping that would help. It didn't. God, but she felt nauseous. "And we moved the bar in here?" How had she wound up in bed with him? Naked yet.

"The bartender cut us off," he told her diplomatically, since technically, she was the only one who had been cut off. "I walked you home."

Her eyes swept over him, stopping just above his hipline. It didn't stop her imagination from going further.

"And didn't keep walking," she concluded.

"No." He couldn't gauge her voice. Was she asking questions, or was there an accusation building? "Is any of what happened last night coming back to you?" He was specifically hoping for the part where she had thrown herself at him. There was no tactful way to make a reference to that. And besides, he still felt he was to blame despite everything.

It was coming back. In flashing bits and pieces, like the view through a kaleidoscope that was swiftly rolling down a hill. And then, suddenly, it all came back to her in its entirety.

Sarajane's mouth dropped opened and she looked at him. Oh, how could she? How *could* she? "I threw myself at you."

Jordan shrugged carelessly, trying to divert the blame. "More or less," he allowed. "I did try to stop you."

Sarajane was trying very hard not to look at him. But it was an utterly losing battle. The man did have a magnificent physique. Warmth began to spread through her with long, probing fingers, reaching out to every part of her.

Embarrassed by what she was feeling, she said, "Obviously not hard enough."

"No," he agreed. "Not hard enough." His eyes swept over her face. "But no court in the world would convict me of that one."

She had no idea why that statement should make her feel as warm as it did. Or why, given the circumstances, all she could think of was not getting into her clothes and putting all this behind her, but of making love with Jordan, this time so she could remember every detail clearly.

"Maybe yes, maybe no," she allowed, slipping back down on the bed as she made the pronouncement. "What we need to do is go over the evidence, very carefully, just in case we can find a loophole."

He had never known, Jordan thought as he slid

down beside her in the bed and took her into his arms, that background research could be nearly so satisfying or entertaining.

Chapter Thirteen

The night of lovemaking with Sarajane did not wipe out the sting of his first courtroom loss, but Jordan had to admit that it certainly helped soften it. Although no one would have ever accused him of being a monk, he felt as if he'd just been going through the motions this last year or so.

That feeling had been absent last night.

And this morning.

Making love with Sarajane had been a unique experience. Instead of leaving him satisfied, it had left him wanting more. He hadn't felt that way since he'd first been initiated into this wondrous world of sex and women.

He finally left her at six to go to his own apartment to shower and change. When he saw her again at eight, at the agency, he felt like a high-school kid reacting to his first crush. The trip back through time was exhilarating.

As long as he didn't think outside the box, or beyond the following Friday. Because the Monday after that was the day when he would revert back to being a high-priced attorney affiliated with a prestigious law firm. He would be back in his world and Sarajane would remain here, in hers. Given what his life had been like before he stepped through Advocate Aid's doors, he knew that there was little to no chance of their being together or even having their paths cross.

But until then, he decided abruptly as a trail of Sarajane's perfume drifted toward him as she moved past his desk, there was no reason why they couldn't enjoy one another.

The man at his desk who was baring his soul to him stopped for a breath. Jordan held up his hand, signaling a momentary break. Catching hold of Sarajane's wrist, he drew her attention to him. "Are you free for dinner?"

Lost in thoughts that had much more to do with him than the folders she was carrying back to her desk, Sarajane looked at him with a slightly bemused expression on her face. Time had a way of getting lost here. "It's only eleven-thirty. That's more like lunch."

"Tonight," Jordan clarified. "Are you up for dinner tonight?"

The bemused expression gave way to a warm smile. Something stirred inside his chest. He was too old, too experienced to feel this way. And yet, he did, he thought in amazement.

"Sure." Sarajane thought for a moment. There was this fancy recipe she'd been wanting to try. Cooking for just herself always felt like a waste, but now that Jordan was coming over, she had the perfect excuse. "I can stop at the grocery store on the way home—"

Jordan was shaking his head before she finished. He wanted to wow her. To make up for last night by wining and dining her properly. And then, perhaps, the rest would take care of itself, he added silently. The knot in his stomach tightened in anticipation.

"I was thinking more along the lines of taking you out to a restaurant." He knew just the one—if he could wangle a reservation. Chez Pierre was usually booked solid weeks in advance, but the owner owed him a favor. The man's daughter had been facing a shoplifting charge and he had not only successfully gotten her off, but had had the charge expunged from her record as well. The man told him he was in his debt for life. Jordan figured a table for two was a reasonable exchange.

Her smile widened. This would give her a chance to wear that slinky black dress she kept in the back of her closet. "Sounds great," she told Jordan.

The man at Jordan's desk squirmed. "Can we get back to my case now, please? I've got to get back to work soon."

"Absolutely," Jordan answered cheerfully. Funny how her smile made him feel lighter than air, he thought, doing his best to turn his attention back to a feud over a bulldog.

"Hey, hey, hey, what do you thinking you're doing?" Eric Logan asked sharply as he crossed the master bedroom in record time, presenting himself directly in front of the king-sized bed he shared with his wife.

Jenny swung her legs out from beneath the covers, digging her knuckles into the mattress for support. Her whole world had shrunk to this bed and she was swiftly growing to hate it.

"I'm blowing this Popsicle stand," she announced with bravado. She was so weary of resting she could have screamed. "And getting up before I forget how to use my legs."

Eric patiently tucked her legs back under the covers, foiling her attempts to flee what she had come to regard as her soft prison.

"You won't forget, Jen," he assured her. "I have faith in you. Doctor said complete bed rest, remember?"

Rolling her eyes, she bit back an exasperated retort. "How can I forget? You and everyone else you hired to keep tabs on me keep reminding me." She looked up at him, a pleading look in her eyes. "Eric, I can't live like this any more."

It had only been a couple of weeks. Less, he thought, calculating the actual time lapsed. "It's just for a few months, honey." He took her hand in his. Funny how he had never realized how fragile she was. When he thought about the possibility that he could lose her, he could hardly breathe. "Trust me, this'll be over in no time. You'll be looking back and wondering why you didn't just enjoy having nothing to do."

Her expression told him that would never happen. "I wasn't made to do nothing," she insisted. She looked around at all the things spread out on the bed that were meant to divert her. She was surrounded by books, her laptop, the newspaper, and all she wanted to do was put them in an orderly stack and get on with her life. "Eric, I'm going crazy."

"I could pick up some new books for you on my way home," he offered. That went over like a lead balloon. "Books on tape, video games, DVDs—you name it, I'll bring it."

She only wanted one thing. "Let me get up and go back to my life." She knew Eric meant well. He'd even hired a nanny to watch Cole. The woman was lovely, but she just wanted to be there with Cole herself. Wanted to get back to doing something useful and meaningful instead of growing roots into a mattress.

The love of her life shook his head. "No can do,

honey." Sitting down beside her on the bed, Eric kissed the top of her head and slipped his arm around her shoulders. He caressed the swell of her stomach with his other hand. "That's an important little passenger you're carrying around with you. You don't want to risk anything happening to the baby, do you?"

"No." Jenny looked back at the article that had set her off this morning. "But I'm thinking of other babies."

He laughed. That was his Jenny, always planning ahead. "Let's have this one first, honey, and then we'll talk."

She stared at him for a moment, and then realized that he thought she meant having more babies of their own. "No, I mean the babies at the Children's Connection. Just look at this."

Incensed, she pulled over a section of the *Gazette* and held it up for him. The story was on page three, where it had been running for the last two weeks. How many different ways were there to say the same thing? And why did the reporters feel they had to drag up past scandals? Why couldn't they give the organization a break after all the good that it had done?

"The media is beating this thing about Robbie to death." She tossed the paper aside like the gossip rag she felt it was. "All the good work that your family's done is being undone just like that." She pressed her lips together to keep the more heated words back. The baby didn't need to be privy to that. Still, when she thought of what was being said and done in the name of journalism she could hardly stand it. "Did you know that Robbie resigned?" Her heart ached for her oldest brother-in-law. "That place meant the world to him."

They were alike that way, she and Robbie. Both felt a certain degree of affection for the organization that allowed so many childless couples to have the family they always longed for.

Anger flickered in her eyes. "If he resigned, it was because he was hounded into doing it. All this bad publicity could ruin the organization," she lamented. "And then where would all those people go? And what about the children?"

Eric held his hands up to stop her before she really got wound up. "You're preaching to the choir, honey."

He took the paper from her and glanced at the story she was referring to. Frowning, he tossed the paper aside, purposely out of Jenny's reach. As angry as he was for what this was doing to the brother he felt deserved better after all he'd been through, he was more concerned about his wife. She didn't need this kind of hype upsetting her. He paused for a moment, casting about for a way to handle this.

"Maybe they could do with the services of a good public relations firm," he said, thinking out loud. Jenny lit up like a Christmas tree.

"That's perfect. Do you know any PR firms?"

Funny she should mention that, he thought. "I

know of one. My cousin LJ runs a very successful PR firm in New York City."

Jenny's eyes narrowed as she looked at him. She thought she'd met his entire family, but this was a new name on her. "You have a cousin LJ? You never mentioned him."

"I have a whole mess of cousins I never mentioned," he told her. He supposed now was as good a time as any to tell her. "Six to be exact." He saw her eyes widen even more. "LJ, Ryan who's an architect, Jake, a doctor and Scott, a private investigator. There's also Suzie and Janet."

"Suzie and Janet," she echoed.

He nodded. "They're my half-cousins, I guess. They belong to Lawrence's second wife, Abigail. His first wife, Lisanne, died about ten years ago."

Jenny did her best to assimilate the information flowing her way. They'd been married for three years. Why hadn't he ever mentioned these people before? And why hadn't they been at the wedding? "Where've you been hiding them?"

"Not me—" he was quick to explain "—my dad. He has this younger brother, Lawrence, they haven't talked for thirty years—"

She found that hard to believe. Terrance Logan had always been so kind to her. "But your father's such a nice man—"

"No argument." In an odd sort of way, one had nothing to do with the other as far as his father was concerned. "The way I heard it, Uncle Lawrence and Dad had the usual typical sibling rivalry when they were kids. My dad was the one who wound up inheriting the Logan Corporation and he was a bit of a stickler when it came to the business, always finding fault with the way Lawrence did things. My dad lived and breathed the company in the early days. Lawrence believed in the stop-and-smell-the-roses philosophy.

"They grew further apart. Lawrence went his own way and became a psychologist. He made it big with a self-help book in the eighties—*The Most Important Thing,*" he recalled the title for her.

Jenny nodded. The book sounded vaguely familiar, one of those bestsellers that enters into the public's consciousness and remains there. "I think I've heard of that."

He nodded. "A lot of people have. It was about finding meaning in your life outside of the ordinary materialistic trappings. It did very well. Trouble was, one of the examples Lawrence used to personify the kind of driven life he was demonizing turned out to be a not-too-fictionalized version of my father.

"Dad saw it as an indictment of everything he'd accomplished. They had a huge falling-out over the book and haven't spoken since, although Lawrence tried to establish contact with my Dad when Robbie was found. But my father wouldn't hear of it." Eric sighed. He had a great deal of respect for his father and all that he had accomplished, but he was aware of the man's shortcomings as well. "He can be very stubborn when it comes to his pride."

You learn something every day, Jenny thought. "So it would seem." Since there was no sense in dwelling on the past, she focused on the immediate problem. "You think this LJ will talk to you?"

He was pretty certain that there'd be no difficulty in reestablishing a connection. "We've been in contact over the years. Mom didn't think we should be cut off from an entire branch of the family just because of Dad's pride. Of course, Dad doesn't know about this—"

Jenny laughed. "How about that? Intrigue, right here under my nose."

Eric couldn't resist touching the tip of her nose. "More like an upscale soap opera," he amended.

"So you'll call him?" she asked eagerly. She knew she'd feel a lot better if something was done to help out the Children's Connection. She'd still be bedridden, but at least things would be getting done. "This secret cousin of yours?"

Eric rose to his feet again. "Right after I get to work."

She knew he had a way of getting distracted. "Promise?" she pressed.

He looked down at her pointedly. "If you promise to stay put."

She'd known that was coming. "I promise."

It wasn't that he didn't trust her, he just knew how

antsy she felt. "Dorothy will tell me if you try to make a break for it." Dorothy was the housekeeper he had hired the day he discovered Jenny was pregnant.

She shook her head, resigned. "Snitches, under my own roof."

He placed a hand affectionately on her shoulder. "Everyone just worries about you, Jen."

"Go. Call." Jenny waved him out of the room.

Eric stopped only long enough to quickly kiss her goodbye and then he was gone.

True to his word, as soon as he walked into his office, Eric instructed his assistant to look up LJ's PR firm in New York City.

Less than an hour after he'd made Jenny privy to the so-called black-sheep side of his family tree, Eric was on the phone, talking to his oldest cousin. After a few minutes of small talk and catching up, he got down to business and told LJ the reason for the unexpected phone call.

Eric pulled no punches and told him everything that had been going on with the agency. The mix-up with the embryos, the fact that black-market-baby trafficking had been suspected, etc. He left nothing out.

"I know this might be kind of awkward for you because the Children's Connection is very dear to my mother and both my parents have given a great deal of money to the organization over the years. If you don't want to take this on because of personal reasons, just say the word. I'll understand. All I ask is a decent referral."

"No referral necessary," LJ assured him in his easy voice. "The personal problems exist between your father and mine, not you and me. This is the twenty-first century and the Hatfields and the McCoys are just a legend in some forgotten history book. There's no need to carry on a blood feud." Eric heard his cousin laugh quietly at the term. "Bottom line, turning the public's opinion around about the agency sounds like one hell of a challenge and I have always lived for challenges. How soon do you need me out there?"

Eric laughed. This was turning out to be almost too easy for words. "How soon can you be here?"

There was a pause on the other end of the line and Eric thought he heard the sound of LJ typing on a keyboard. His cousin was back on the line in less than two minutes. "I've got a few things to see to first. How does Monday sound?"

Eric had been prepared for a lot longer lag than that. "Monday's great."

"Okay, then it's a deal. Monday it is. I'll get back to you once my assistant has my travel plans in place."

If only all his problems were that easily taken care of, Eric thought. "I really appreciate this, LJ."

"Hey, we're family, right? No matter what the old men say." LJ sounded as if he genuinely believed what he was saying. "See you soon."

"Soon," Eric echoed and smiled to himself as he hung up the receiver. Wait until he called Jenny with this. That should put the sparkle back in her eyes. At least temporarily.

Sarajane sighed. This day seemed to drag on forever. She thought that last person who had brought her plight to Jordan would never leave. She'd monopolized him for almost two hours. Every time it looked as if the woman was winding up, she brought out another crumpled piece of paper to show him, another issue about her eviction that she felt needed addressing. She became very agitated as she talked about the wrongs she'd endured.

In the end, although she became increasingly disgruntled, Jordan managed to convince her that there was really nothing the agency could do for her, other than give her the name of a reputable shelter. After examining every piece of mail she brought him, Jordan had to conclude that the landlord had been within his rights to evict her. Jordan pointed out that the man had been kinder than most, allowing her to stay on almost six months without paying. As tactfully as he could, Jordan pointed out that she had clearly been taking advantage of the landlord's generosity.

The one thing he did wind up doing for her, after placing a few phone calls, was to get the charge of disorderly conduct against her dismissed. This, even though she had resisted the marshals who came to remove her from the premises, spitting in one of their faces.

Jordan promised to get back to her if anything came up in her favor. And with that, he escorted her to the door, making sure to close and lock it after he'd all but coaxed her to the other side.

Just before he did, he slipped a hundred-dollar bill into her hand. He closed the door just as the woman looked as if she was going to kiss him.

Sarajane watched him as he walked back to his desk. Everyone else had left for the night. Everyone but her and the man she'd slept with.

The man she'd slept with. The sentence echoed back to her.

She shouldn't be going out with him again, she told herself. She shouldn't be setting herself up for the eventual disappointment that would come all too soon. A disappointment she knew was coming because in less than two weeks he was going back to his high-priced world, leaving her to deal with the evictees and the people with pending lawsuits and cases against them they knew nothing about.

Oh, c'mon, live a little. Cinderella knew she had a curfew, it didn't keep her from going to the ball. And look how that turned out.

Cinderella was a fairy tale. There would be no fairy-tale ending for her. There wouldn't even be a consolation prize of a pair of glass slippers, not that she'd ever understood how anyone could walk in those.

But there'd be memories. Good ones, the little voice in her head whispered. Or was that in her heart?

She'd seen him slip the money to the woman and it had gladdened her heart, making her even more vulnerable to the man than she already was.

Still watching Jordan, Sarajane did her best to block out the little voice, but for some reason, she couldn't silence it, couldn't drown it out even when she started thinking of a particularly infectious lyric to a song that had been stuck in her head just the other day. Nothing helped. The little hopeful voice managed to triumph over it all.

"Ready to go?" Jordan turned from his desk as the computer screen finally darkened and then disappeared. "To the restaurant," he added when Sarajane didn't seem to know what he was referring to.

This is where you do the right thing and turn him down. "I've got to go home and change first." So much for the right thing.

Jordan was already crossing over to her. He shook his head.

"No time," he told her, taking her hand. "We've got about fifteen minutes to get there. If we're not right on time, the owner gets petulant. Worse than that, he gives away our table. Besides—" he grinned at her "—you look great."

Because he gave her hand a little tug, she rose to her feet. "For haunting houses," she retorted.

His hand to the small of her back, he escorted her

to the rear of the office and the exit. "A little sideline never hurt." Her eyes widened in surprise and he laughed. Didn't she know he was kidding? "C'mon, Sarajane, if it ain't broke, don't fix it."

She wasn't sure if he was just repeating some hardware-store mantra, or if he actually meant what he said. No, it couldn't be the former, she decided. She sincerely doubted if Jordan Hall had ever even seen the inside of a hardware store, or picked up a screwdriver, or worked with his hands outside of a bedroom for that matter.

Two different worlds, Sarajane reminded herself. They were from two completely different worlds. But for the next week and a half, maybe she could pretend that they weren't.

"Okay," she said cheerfully, getting out the key to lock the back door. "Let's go."

Chapter Fourteen

The evening didn't end in the restaurant when dinner was over. Sarajane had known that it wouldn't. The moment she'd said yes to Jordan's invitation that morning, she knew they would wind up in bed together.

She just hadn't thought of whose bed.

It was his.

The huge, king-sized bed in the master suite that lay at the far side of his penthouse apartment. Try as she might not to, she found herself comparing the two beds. Comparing their worlds: his apartment, his bed to her tiny twin bed in her tiny bedroom within her tiny fifth-floor apartment, which half the time turned into a fifth-floor walk-up because the elevator was malfunctioning for one reason or another.

The experience, she thought, could be likened unto Cinderella spending the night in the palace. For all intents and purposes, it was a fantasy come true. But even in the middle of their wild lovemaking, and it was just that—wild—she could hear a soft little voice whispering in her head: "You don't belong here." Didn't belong in his arms, or in his bed and certainly not in his apartment.

But, oh, it felt so wonderful while it was happening that she just couldn't make herself do the right thing, couldn't find a way to protect herself. Couldn't get up and leave before she was completely and hopelessly forever lost.

Who was she kidding? Sarajane upbraided herself. That boat had sailed. She *was* lost, it was just a matter of how lost. And what she could do to get herself back in her own harbor without sustaining too much damage to her poor heart.

"A penny for your thoughts," Jordan murmured against her hair as he gathered Sarajane in closer to him.

They were in bed together and the afterglow of lovemaking had yet to dissipate. He found himself hoping it would linger on a little longer. This was the third night he'd brought Sarajane to his penthouse after a mind-draining long day at the agency and somehow, it was beginning to feel as if he'd been doing this forever. As if having her in his life, in his bed, was something that had been going on for a very long time instead of merely a handful of nights.

Sarajane looked at him, unaware that she had drifted off. A tingling sensation slithered through her as he pressed a kiss to her bare shoulder. This man could turn her on as easily as she could throw a light switch.

"So that's how your family made its fortune, by being cheap," she quipped.

Jordan raised her hair from her neck, lightly skimming his tongue along her skin. He liked the way she shivered in response.

"We prefer to think of it as frugal, and, in light of inflation, I'll up the asking price to a nickel." He let her hair fall back into place. "How's that?"

She laughed softly in response, struggling against a bittersweet sensation. *Oh, I'm going to miss this.* "Spoken like a true lawyer."

"I am what I am." And then, as he looked at her again, his teasing tone faded. "What's on your mind, Sarajane?"

She didn't want to let him in. This was too personal, too painful. She didn't want Jordan thinking of her as being needy. Hell, she didn't like thinking of herself in that way.

"What makes you think there's something on my mind?"

He'd sensed her distraction and wanted to know if something was bothering her. Wanted to know, he realized, about everything that had anything to do with her.

"You were somewhere else tonight. This part of you—" he lightly tapped her temple "—wasn't here."

Because that part of me was worrying about a week from now. Wondering who would take my place in this bed with you.

But she couldn't say that, couldn't allow Jordan to think that she was being jealous when she had no right to be. She knew that this was nothing more than a pleasant interlude for him. The best she could hope for was to leave some sort of an impression on him that he would recall fondly once he had returned to a life already in progress…

Because Jordan was waiting for some sort of reply, she plucked the first thing she could think of out of the air. Something that concerned them both and sounded plausible.

"I was just thinking about Alicia. She's taking care of Joe's kids," she told him in case he wasn't aware of that. "She thought it was only temporary. Now she doesn't know what to think."

Sarajane was like Jenny, he thought. Utterly selfless. How did someone get to be that noble? he wondered in awe.

He did his best to reassure her. "This isn't over yet," he promised, wrapping his arm around her waist. "I've got appeals in the works." He'd made sure to put through all the paperwork immediately.

To reassure her, he repeated what he'd told her earlier. "And I'm going to get to the bottom of why Joe suddenly did a one-eighty and claimed that he wasn't innocent when he'd maintained the opposite up until just before the trial." He saw the bemused expression on her face. Had he said something to confuse her? To amuse her? "What?"

Sarajane had heard only one thing. "You're appealing his case?"

He'd thought that was a given. Why was she so surprised? "Yes, why?"

An appeal wasn't something that came around just by snapping your fingers. Everything related to the law moved at an anemic snail's pace. "But that's going to take time."

He didn't see her point. "I know."

Was she missing something? "You're scheduled to go back to your ivory tower at the end of next week."

He wondered if she'd meant that to be insulting, or if it was just the way she thought about the world he came from. "I know that. We have phones, Sarajane. I can keep tabs on the appeal from there."

Why was he doing this? He was under no obligation to follow up on anything once he left. "He still can't pay you."

Did she think he didn't know that? "I'm still not asking." He could see she wanted more than that. "It wouldn't hurt Morrison and Treherne to do a little pro bono work once in a while." Damn, but sitting here next to her like this was making him want her all over again. Leaning in against her, he outlined the shell of her ear with his tongue. Man did not live on work alone. "Enough shop talk for the night."

Already the warmth was pouring through her veins like hot honey. "My thoughts exactly."

Sarajane groaned as she realized that she'd almost drowned her hot dog in hot mustard. Taking a napkin, she tried to do a little damage control. She could feel Alicia watching her skeptically.

This was the first time she'd managed to get together with the nurse since the trial had ended and they were grabbing a bite of fast food at a lunch wagon that habitually parked halfway between the Children's Connection and Advocate Aid. It was about all either of them could afford to spend.

"I think I'm falling in love with him," Sarajane lamented in response to Alicia's quizzical look.

It was Monday and Friday was coming fast. Too fast. Like a potential victim aware that she was standing directly in the path of a hurricane, Sarajane still couldn't get herself to shore up her beaches and prepare for what was coming. A part of her was hoping for a miracle.

"And this is a bad thing because?" Alicia asked, glad to be focusing on someone else's problems for a change instead of on what was happening to her brother. "The man is rich, handsome and it's easy to see that he's really crazy about you." The couple of times she'd witnessed Jordan and her friend interacting, she was extremely aware of the sexual tension, the sparks that were all but shooting between them.

"The operative word being *crazy*," Sarajane agreed. "As I would be if I thought this had a snowball's chance in hell of going anywhere."

Alicia didn't ask what *this* referred to. She could read between the lines. She frowned at Sarajane. "Why are you so negative?"

Oh, for so many reasons. "Past experience." Alicia knew about Rocco and about Andrew even though she and Sarajane hadn't been friends at the time. Sarajane had given the nurse a thumbnail sketch of life with both. "And besides, our two worlds don't mesh."

Alicia looked unfazed. "So create a third one that's the best of both." She stopped eating and looked at her friend. "Honey, do you know how hard it is to find someone to care about who cares about you in return?"

Sarajane stubbornly refused to let herself believe what Alicia was obviously buying into: that she was destined for a fairy-tale ending. "The man has taken me out to eat several times and we've gone to bed together. That doesn't instantly translate into true love."

"And he rescued you," Alicia reminded her suddenly, holding up her index finger as she made the point. "Don't forget that he rescued you with no small danger to himself."

Sarajane could feel her eyes watering—not from anything that Alicia said, but because the mustard was too spicy. She sniffed, wiping away one loose tear. "What are you, his agent?"

Alicia gave her arm a squeeze. "No, I'm the impartial bystander you were hoping for when you put this in my lap. Now eat up." She nodded at the half-eaten hot dog Sarajane was holding. "I've got to be getting back."

Sarajane looked at her watch. How had that happened? "Oh, God, so do I." Wrapping a napkin around what was left of her so-called lunch, she stuffed it into her shoulder bag. "I'll take a rain check for the rest of this conversation."

"Coward," Alicia commented, gathering her things together. "Just remember, there are worse things in life than having a sexy, naked man in your bed."

"His bed," Sarajane corrected, already putting distance between them.

"*Any* bed," Alicia called after her.

Sarajane just waved her hand at Alicia without looking back. She had no time to get into a discussion over this right now.

"Four more days and you're a free man," Eric commented. The sound of his voice echoed within the room where they had met for their weekly racquetball game. Because of a scheduling conflict, they were playing on a Monday instead of the previous Friday.

"Yeah." Funny, freedom didn't feel as good as he'd anticipated at the beginning of all this. Jordan lunged for the shot that Eric sent his way. It went whistling by the rim of his racket.

Eric was surprised. "You missed that by a mile. My game hasn't improved that much." And then it dawned on him. "Something on your mind?"

"No." Jordan knew that he'd fired the denial out too fast, but there was nothing he could do about that. "Jenny find someone to take her place yet?" Which was still temporarily "his" place as well.

Eric shook his head, putting his back into returning the serve. "Not yet."

"Well, I can't stay on," Jordan said with feeling, barely making the shot he reached for. He missed the next one and swallowed a curse.

Eric looked at his brother-in-law thoughtfully. "She's not asking you to. Hell, Jordy, that's the third easy shot you missed. You want to make this game history and just talk for a while?"

Jordan shot him an annoyed look. "I don't need a therapist, Eric."

"Good, because I don't have one in my hip pocket. I do, however, have our friendship to fall back on." For the sake of the game, which he was winning by a mile, he continued playing. But his heart wasn't in it. "You know you can tell me anything."

"Yeah, I know," Jordan agreed as he chased down a shot he would ordinarily have gotten easily. "And

Jenny will hear all about it by the time you make it back to the office."

"Not if you don't want her to," Eric told him seriously. He made a stab at guessing what was bothering his friend. "So this is a Jenny-related subject?"

"No," Jordan retorted, for once hitting the ball squarely. "It's just that you can't keep your mouth shut around my sister."

Eric didn't quite see it in those harsh terms. "Love does that to you. Makes you want to share everything." He hit the ball back to Jordan's half of the court. "But if you want me to keep something secret, I will. You have my word."

Jordan missed the shot and gave up. With a sigh, he dropped his racket and then, leaning against the back wall, he slid down until he was sitting crosslegged on the floor.

What he wanted to do was talk about these feelings he was having, the ones that urged him to climb up on the highest building in Portland and shout her name at the top of his lungs. But he had no idea where to begin, how to frame what was happening to him. So he focused on something else that had been bothering him for the last few days. Something that had been becoming more and more prominent.

He chose his words carefully. "I'm beginning to wonder if maybe I'm wasting my life, working at Morrison and Treherne."

This was a new note, Eric thought, looking at his

brother-in-law. One he wouldn't have expected from Jordan. "Wasting how?"

Jordan scrubbed his hand over his face. Maybe this was a mistake. Maybe he should have kept it all to himself until it was sorted out. "As in getting something meaningful accomplished."

"Keeping rich clients out of jail doesn't do it for you any more?" Eric quipped, his mouth curving. "Rich people need justice, too, Jordy."

Jordan wasn't disputing that. "Agreed, but rich people can afford to get it. If I don't represent some well-to-do man or woman, they can find someone else who can. Easily."

Jordan paused. He was being modest, Eric thought, waiting. When his brother-in-law didn't continue, Eric asked, "What's your point?"

"My point is the people who come to Advocate Aid can't afford to pay for legal aid. Hell, some of them can't afford to pay for food." Until he said it out loud, he hadn't realized just what an impact these last two weeks had had on him, how much of an impact the people he'd dealt with had had on him. He was actually feeling for them. "Justice might be blind, but it costs and if they can't afford attorney fees, they're at the mercy of so many different things in the system."

Eric gauged his friend's tone. He was accustomed to this from Jenny, but this was a side of Jordan he'd never seen before.

"There's always the public defender," he pointed out.

Jordan laughed shortly. "Most of them couldn't care less."

"But you do." It was a simple statement, but it cut to the heart of the matter.

Jordan didn't want to commit to anything out loud. He began to deny it, but that was just an automatic response, not one that came from his gut.

"I don't know," he admitted. He saw a wide grin blossom on Eric's face. "What?"

Eric laid an arm across his shoulders. "Jenny would be so proud of you right now, man."

Jordan shrugged him off. He didn't want this up for discussion. This was just between them. "You promised not to tell her."

Eric raised his hands up, fending off the accusation in Jordan's eyes. "I know, I know, and I won't, but this would really make her day. Hell, it would make her month. She loves converts."

Jordan bristled. "I didn't say I was a convert. I'm just having…thoughts on the subject," he finally said.

Eric's grin showed no signs of fading away. "According to Jenny, that's how being selfless and dedicated to a nobler cause than buying the next pair of designer shoes usually starts."

Jordan sighed. He should have just kept his mouth shut. By this time next week, life would be back to normal and all this would be moot. He ignored the unexpected pang in his gut and glanced at his watch. It was later than he thought.

Getting to his feet, he said, "I've got to be getting back."

"Anything else on your mind?" Eric wanted to know, picking up both their rackets. Handing Jordan's to him, Eric followed him out of the room.

For just a single moment, Jordan was tempted. Tempted to ask Eric that all-important question: When did he first know he was in love with Jenny? But asking that would open a door on a subject he had absolutely no desire to get into. An avalanche of questions would follow. And then Eric would tell Jenny no matter *what* he'd promised.

So he shook his head and summoned his most innocent voice. "Not a thing."

Lawrence Logan always felt that his emotions were much too close to the surface, more suited to a feminine disposition than to one belonging to a man.

Simply put, he was far too sentimental for his own good.

Right now, he felt emotion all but choking him as he sat in his living room, looking upon all four of his sons. It had been a long time since his boys had been gathered together under one roof like this. Grown, they had gone their separate ways to pursue their lives. All had been successful in their chosen fields and he was proud of each and every one of them.

But he had to admit, in the secret recesses of his heart, that he missed the years when they were young. When they had all been beneath one roof, living within the sound of his voice and he within the sound of theirs. Life had been simpler then. And in many ways, richer.

He supposed, in an odd sort of way, he had his brother Terrance to thank for this, or at least one of his older brother's offspring.

LJ, his oldest son, had flown all the way from the East Coast to see if he could find a way to break the Children's Connection's freefall, saving its reputation before it ultimately crashed and burned. He'd read that Terrence was involved with the organization. According to the article he'd skimmed, it was near and dear to his brother's heart.

This was presupposing that Terrence actually still had one of those.

Lawrence banished the cynical thought. It wasn't worthy of him and it had no place at this gathering tonight.

But he couldn't banish his concern quite so easily.

"Be careful," he said to LJ without preamble, interrupting a conversation the latter was having with Scott, the youngest male in the family.

LJ looked at him uncertainly, confused. This had come out of the blue. "Dad?"

Lawrence backtracked. "When you deal with the Children's Connection, be careful. Your uncle Terrence likes to find fault with people and he's not a very forgiving man, trust me on that." There was no point in rehashing the origins of the feud, or how Terrence had refused all of his attempts at a reconciliation. It would sound too much like badmouthing his brother.

"I'll be dealing with Uncle Terrence's son, Eric, or rather his wife," LJ pointed out. "He's the one who called me, but according to Eric, she's the one who's really concerned about the effects of all the bad press the organization has been getting."

His son's words did nothing to negate Lawrence's feelings on the matter. "Son, wife, they all belong to that side of the family."

It sounded so melodramatic. LJ did his best not to grin. "I forget, Dad," he deadpanned. "Is 'that side' the good side or the bad side?"

"It's just *that* side," Lawrence replied. "And it will save you a great deal of grief to remember that you belong to *our* side." With that, he rose from the sofa and looked at his other sons. He nodded at the goblets on the coffee table, most of which, he noted, were empty. "Can I interest anyone in a refill?"

Several hands went up.

Chapter Fifteen

When he had initially undertaken this reluctant good deed for Jenny's sake, Jordan had felt as if he was standing on the wrong side of an interminable jail sentence. He'd thought of the three weeks in terms of minutes, seconds even, dribbling by at an incredibly slow pace. The "sentence" was something to survive and eventually put behind him—with relief.

Now, facing the other side of those three weeks, the last few minutes of the last day, Jordan had to admit that he had never known three weeks to go by so quickly. There just didn't seem to be enough time to get to everything, certainly not enough time to make a dent in the case load that still remained piled up on his desk.

Not his desk, he silently corrected himself, Jenny's desk. And the desk of whoever it was that came after him to carry on in Jenny's name until such time as she was back on her feet again.

But whoever's desk it was, the case load still remained, each folder belonging to a different person, a different complaint, a different cause.

Strictly speaking, the pace here might have been very close to the one he experienced working at Morrison and Treherne. But that was where the similarity ended.

The people he'd been seeing these last three weeks lived from paycheck to paycheck, their closets were not bulging with clothing bearing designer labels. They did without so that their children could have a few of the amenities that the world he came from took completely for granted. If these people were taken advantage of and had no money to pay someone to speak on their behalf, it was just something else they had to endure.

Not his problem, he told himself. He'd never felt guilty before because he'd been born well off, because his was a life of affluence. But then, he thought, he'd never been in the trenches before, never seen life from the other side before. It did make a difference.

And so, he'd like to think, had he during his stay here. But now it was time to withdraw, to go back to the life that was waiting for him.

His life.

As Eric had said, he reminded himself, rich people needed representation, too. And why shouldn't he make top dollar for his talent? He'd earned the right, having studied hard and put in his time.

Jordan automatically went through the motions of shutting down for the night. Except that this time, it wasn't just for the night, or the weekend, it was permanent.

As he packed up, he watched Sarajane escort his last client out. The woman was a single mother whose recently remarried ex-husband, an insurance broker, was trying to win custody of their daughter. The woman, Anita Quinn, felt her ex was only doing it to hurt her, not because he loved the little girl. But he was well off and she, a former housewife with a minimum-wage job, was not. Donald Quinn's lawyer was using everything in the book to make his ex-wife out to be a bad mother whose child would be better off with the stability and advantages that he and his new wife could give her.

Someone else was going to have to handle that, Jordan told himself sternly. He wasn't going to be here. Granted, he'd decided to hang on to Joe Juarez's case, but there was a limit to what Morrison and Treherne would agree to allow him to do.

The front door locked, Sarajane turned and walked back toward him. He liked the way she moved, he thought. Half poetry, half raw determination. And all woman.

She stopped walking when she came to his desk. "So," she said. The single word hung between them, waiting to be joined by more or used as a turning point.

"So," he echoed, suddenly at a loss for anything else to say. So many emotions were ricocheting inside of him, he couldn't begin to harness them or even get a handle on them.

She took a breath and released it before continuing. "Bet you're glad this is over with."

He wasn't sure he understood where she was going with this. "You mean today?"

Sarajane shook her head. "No, I mean this whole thing." She gestured around the room. He was going to miss the way she talked with her hands, underscoring her words. "Your stint here."

She felt awkward.

Worse, she felt like crying. All day she'd felt as if she'd been on a death watch, waiting for that last moment, the one when he walked out that door.

And out of her life.

They were a package, she and Advocate Aid. Once Jordan walked away from one, he'd be walking away from the other. She was certain he knew that.

Her throat felt scratchy as she fought to hold back the tears. She'd be damned if she'd let him see her cry. "For what it's worth, you were a great help."

He smiled faintly at her words. "Jenny will be glad to hear that."

"She'd be gladder to hear that you stayed on."

Damn it, how had that escaped? She'd promised herself not to say anything like that, not to ask, not to hint that he remain. Oh God, was that pity in his eyes? She felt her back going up.

"Sarajane, I can't."

"I know," she fairly snapped, backtracking. Distancing herself from him. "I'm not asking you to, I'm just saying that would be what Jenny would want." She raised her eyes to his. "But then, you can't always have what you want, can you?"

"No," he agreed quietly. "You can't." He paused for a moment, trying not to think about how much he was going to miss seeing her weaving her way through the small office every day. Miss bumping into her because the space was so crammed. Miss her. Impulse had him saying, "Come home with me, Sarajane."

She wanted to. God, but she wanted to. But what would that accomplish? Give her a few more hours with him? And then what? It would still be over. He would still be leaving. It was better all around, for both of them, if there was a clean break.

"I can't." When he looked as if he was going ask why, she added, "I promised a friend I'd be over at their place at eight."

He heard the finality in her voice. He'd never been one to push, even though this time, he wanted to with a fierceness that was all but overwhelming.

"Oh."

There was no friend and she didn't know what she would have said if he asked for details. But Jordan didn't press, so she was spared trying to fabricate more of a lie.

And because he didn't press, she knew that she'd been right to lie in the first place. Because he was only going through the motions asking her to come home with him. The only thing on his mind was getting in one more night of hot sex, nothing more. If there had been anything more, he would have asked her to change her plans, or volunteered to wait until she had met her obligation. People who cared were willing to snatch tiny shards of time with the person they cared about.

But Jordan had said nothing.

Because he didn't care.

She shifted impatiently, wanting this to be over before she did something really stupid. Like change her mind and go home with him. "Look, I want to lock up, so, are you ready to go?"

"Yeah."

He rose and she found that she was standing much too close. Their bodies were almost touching. More than anything, she wanted to ignore her pride and just throw her arms around him. Just kiss him one more time. Have the world stop turning one more time as he kissed her.

But she'd hate herself in the morning and she knew it.

This is better, that logical little voice told her. She hated that logical little voice.

"Need a ride?" he asked as they walked outside together for the last time.

She shook her head. "Car's still working," she told him. "That mechanic you suggested did a great job."

Each word she said stuck to the roof of her mouth like overly moist peanut butter. She hated small talk. Most of all, she hated him. For making her care again. For making her fall in love.

Abruptly, Sarajane put out her hand. "Well, see you," she said with a cheerfulness that was conspicuously absent from her soul.

He looked down at her hand. What he wanted to do was pull her into his arms and kiss her until they were both numb. What he wanted to do was ask her to come with him, not for the night, but forever.

But he was letting his emotions get the better of him and besides, she'd made it clear that she was severing ties. That she wasn't interested in continuing anything they had.

So he took her hand and shook it. "Yeah, see you," he murmured. Dropping her hand again, he separated himself from her.

She'd lost count of the number of times she'd picked up the receiver, and then put it back into the cradle again, each time battling and overcoming the urge to call Jordan.

She wanted to apologize for being so stiff, so distant on Friday evening. She wanted to rage at him for not doing anything to break down the barriers around her, the barriers that were flimsier than wet paper. She wanted to ask him to really consider coming back to the agency. And if not that, at least to come back to her.

But she didn't call, didn't ask, because she feared hearing a single word in reply: *No.* And even if he didn't reject her, even if he said yes, he'd be doing it because she'd begged, because he'd felt sorry for her. That was no foundation upon which to build a relationship. She would never know what was really in his heart. And there'd always be that fear haunting her that he would hate her for making him feel guilty.

This was better, she told herself, curling up with a half-gallon container of ice cream in front of the TV. An old sitcom episode she knew by heart was on. The familiar. That was comforting somehow.

The sides of the container she held were already beginning to sweat. Moisture slid down the sides like morose tears.

Better never felt so awful.

Jordan frowned as he replaced the receiver on his landline. That was the third invitation to go out this evening that he had turned down. He would have thought, after spending all that time cooped up in that shoebox of an office, he'd be happy to shake the dust off and get back into the swing of things. Get back to the world he'd been born to. The world he knew.

And yet, he had no interest in doing that. No interest in getting together with Belinda, who had called to invite him over for an intimate dinner, or with Patrice who was throwing an impromptu party for "fifty of her closest friends" or even with Kevin Ritchie who, now that Eric was out of the game, had become his designated wingman when they hit parties and sports bars.

He was completely devoid of any desire to socialize, to mingle. To meet women and make love with them.

It was because *she* had infiltrated his head.

Infiltrated it like some damnable virus for which there was no cure. What the hell was wrong with him? He was Jordan Hall, he could have any woman he wanted. He didn't waste time mooning over some petite crusader with a cause. Ever.

And yet…

And yet nothing, he thought, annoyed. It was time to stop acting like some lovestruck adolescent who didn't know which end was up and get his act together. Come Monday morning, he was back to being one of the highest-paid attorneys in Portland, sought after by clients who could afford to pay any price just to have him take on their case.

But that was before he'd lost a case.

To hell with that, he upbraided himself angrily.

That was Sarajane's fault. Everything that was wrong was her fault.

Clinging to that condemnation, Jordan went into his bedroom to change his clothes. As he walked, he took out his cell phone and called Patrice. He felt like going to a party.

Maybe it was her imagination, but the streets felt lonelier somehow this morning.

Driving to the office on Monday, Sarajane was aware of every person loitering on the corners, their faces vacant, without purpose. She was aware of the debris that seemed to be chasing itself in circles here and there along the dirty street. Aware of the empty storefronts that pockmarked the neighborhood and stood like blackened eyes and missing teeth along the blocks.

The sky above was gray.

As gray as her mood.

"Stop it," she upbraided herself out loud, raising her voice over the song on the radio. "Get a grip and get over it. The man was on a vacation. He was slumming. Nothing more. Now it's back to work for him and for you. Back to business as usual. You don't have time to act like some lovesick puppy. There're too many people depending on you."

She knew the office didn't run itself, nor did it run for anyone else who was there. Without her, Harry and Sheldon were completely lost. She was the one who knew where the forms were, who knew the numbers to call no matter what or who was needed. And she was the one who ultimately kept order among the people who crossed their threshold on a daily basis. There was no time to feel sorry for herself and mourn what would never be. She had too much work to do.

Pulling into the lot, Sarajane parked her car directly behind the storefront where Advocate Aid was housed. She got out and locked the vehicle. The lot was empty for the most part. A couple of cars were parked on the far side, but she hardly glanced in that direction. When the area was empty like this, night or day, she'd learned that it was best just to keep walking and get to her destination quickly. The last thing she wanted was to become another statistic. One near-mugging in a lifetime was enough for her.

Sarajane inserted her key in the lock and found that the door was already unlocked. She froze as her heart climbed up in her throat. She was sure she'd locked the door on Friday.

Hadn't she?

But then why was it opened? And why was the security code not engaged? Granted, Harry and Sheldon both knew the code and had their own keys, but she couldn't remember either one of them ever coming in before nine. It was only eight.

Maybe one of them had decided to come in early,

just this once, because now that Jordan was gone, the office was shorthanded again.

Now that Jordan was gone.

The sentence echoed in her head, mocking her. No, she wasn't going to go there again. She'd spent her entire weekend thinking about him, wishing things that didn't have a chance of coming into being. Monday was the beginning of a brand-new week. Time to move on.

The last she'd checked, Jenny was still having no luck landing someone for the short haul. Charity, when it meant giving of yourself rather than from your checkbook, was something that was in very short supply around here, she thought sadly.

Sarajane slowly pushed the back door open, alert to every sound, every movement. There weren't any. *Had* she left the door unlocked? There certainly wasn't anything in here to tempt a burglar.

"Hello?" she called out, still standing in the alcove, within inches of the back door just in case someone had broken in and she had to escape. "Is anyone here?"

"Just us overworked attorneys."

Her breath joined her heart in her throat. That couldn't be—

Refusing to get her hopes up, she nonetheless hurried out of the alcove and into the main room.

It *was* him.

Jordan was sitting at the desk he'd occupied for the last three weeks. Working. Her heart did a cartwheel before she could stop it. She banked down the surge of joy pouring through her.

Something was wrong. There had to be a logical explanation.

Crossing to his desk, she tried to sound distant. It wasn't easy when she had hardly any breath to spare. "What are you doing here?"

He looked up from the file he'd been examining since his arrival more than half an hour ago. In his pocket were the key and the piece of paper with the security code on it that he'd gotten from Jenny last night after he'd come over to tell her his plans.

"A simple 'hello' would have been nice."

"Hello," she echoed numbly, then repeated, "What are you doing here?"

He nodded at the file that was spread out over the desk. "Working on Anita Quinn's case."

The single mother fighting to keep custody of her little girl. It didn't make sense. "Why aren't you at Treherne and Morrison?"

"Morrison and Treherne," he corrected, earning an impatient noise from Sarajane. "Well, for starters, because the file's here, not there."

She wasn't in the mood for any word games. "Jordan, be serious—"

The slightly lopsided grin vanished. "I am serious. Maybe for the first time in my life." He turned his chair from the desk to face her. "I took a leave of absence from the firm."

He'd stayed at Patrice's party for a little more than an hour on Saturday. Being there, listening to inane conversations about which brand of personal water-craft to buy and what exotic resort to fly to for the next vacation had helped him make up his mind. He'd called Jerome Morrison from his car on the way home. It had taken a bit of convincing, but he had skill and his record on his side. "They told me I could come back any time I wanted."

That answered nothing. "*Why* would you take a leave of absence?" Planting a hand on his desk, she leaned over to be closer to his face.

He almost kissed her then. But she deserved an answer to her question. "Because I hate leaving a cluttered desk. And because I hate leaving you in a lurch." He paused for a moment, then said quietly, "And because I hate leaving you."

"I don't understand." She heard someone knocking on the front door. Instead of going to unlock the door and let them in, she ignored the knock. She needed to have this cleared up, and technically, they weren't open for business yet, anyway.

"I don't know how much clearer I can make this." He spread his hands to encompass the room. "I'm where I'm supposed to be." And then he smiled at her, melting her bones just enough to make standing straight a challenge. "I've discovered I have a heart and it seems to be here, so I'm here as well."

No, she wasn't going to jump to conclusions. She

was going to lead with her head, not her heart. "You're talking about the cases."

"The cases. You." He peered at her face. "They kind of go hand in hand, don't they?"

"In a way," she agreed slowly. "So you're here to work."

"Yes. I'm also here because…" She was going to make him say this, wasn't she?

"Yes?"

Blowing out a breath, he pushed back from the desk and rose to his feet. "Damn it, Sarajane, this isn't supposed to be difficult."

He was in her space, but she didn't back away. *"This?"*

Frustrated, he tried to find the right words. "You, me, loving—"

Her eyes opened so wide, they were in danger of falling out. She held up her hand like a traffic cop. "Hold it. Back up. Are you telling me—"

"That I love you? Yes." He felt like a man on a tightrope strung out over Niagara Falls. So far, he was doing this on faith because she hadn't said anything in kind to him. "And at the risk of being completely shot down, I'm asking you to—"

She threw her arms around him and cried, "Yes!"

He looked at her, a little stunned. "Yes?"

She nodded, fighting hard to keep tears from falling. In the background, the person at the front door was knocking again, with more feeling this time. "Yes!"

Jordan laughed as relief flooded him. He wrapped his arms around her. "You don't even know what the question is."

"I don't care." It didn't matter. He wanted her, she *knew* he wanted her. "The answer's yes."

"You have got a lot to learn about negotiations," he told her fondly.

I love you, Jordan Hall. It's about time you came to your senses. "That's for divorces, I'm assuming that's not where this is headed."

He raised his voice as the knocking grew louder still. "No, it's headed down the aisle if you still mean what you just shouted."

"More than ever."

He didn't want her to feel pressured into anything. He would wait if she needed time. "You're sure?"

"Oh, I'm sure." There was absolutely no doubt in her mind. "You've had my number, Jordan Hall, from the first moment you set foot in here." The knocking at the door had become so insistent, the front window was rattling. "I guess I'd better let him in before he knocks down the door."

"In a minute," he told her, still holding her against him and showing no signs of releasing her. "First, I want to hear you say it."

"Say what?" And then she smiled. "That I love you? I thought you knew."

"Whether I did or not is not the question," he told her. "Some things you just have to hear for yourself."

She smiled up into his eyes. "I love you, Jordan Hall. How's that?"

"Good. Again."

She nodded obligingly. "I—"

She didn't get a chance to finish. Given a choice between talking and kissing, there was no contest. Kissing always won.

Just like Jordan.

* * * * *

Turn the page for a sneak preview of
IF I'D NEVER KNOWN YOUR LOVE
by
Georgia Bockoven

From the brand-new series
Harlequin Everlasting Love
Every great love has a story to tell.™

There's no way for you to know this, Evan, but I haven't written to you for a few months. Actually, it's been almost a year. I had a hard time picking up a pen once more after we paid the second ransom and then received a letter saying it wasn't enough. I was so sure you were coming home that I took the kids along to Bogotá so they could fly home with you and me, something I swore I'd never do. I've fallen in love with Colombia and the people who've opened their hearts to me. But fear is a constant companion when I'm there. I won't ever expose our children to that kind of danger again.

I'm at a loss over what to do anymore, Evan. I've begged and pleaded and thrown temper tantrums with every official I can corner both here and at home. They've been incredibly tolerant and understanding, but in the end as ineffectual as the rest of us.

I try to imagine what your life is like now, what you do every day, what you're wearing, what you eat. I want to believe that the people who have you are misguided yet kind, that they treat you well. It's how I survive day to day. To think of you being mistreated hurts too much. If I picture you locked away somewhere and suffering, a weight descends on me that makes it almost impossible to get out of bed in the morning.

Your captors surely know you by now. They have to recognize what a good man you are. I imagine you working with their children, telling them that you have children, too, showing them the pictures you carry in your wallet. Can't the men who have you understand how much your children miss you? How can it not matter to them?

How can they keep you away from us all this

time? Over and over, we've done what they asked. Are they oblivious to the depth of their cruelty? What kind of people are they that they don't care?

I used to keep a calendar beside our bed next to the peach rose you picked for me before you left. Every night I marked another day, counting how many you'd been gone. I don't do that any longer. I don't want to be reminded of all the days we'll never get back.

When I can't sleep at night, I tell you about my day. I imagine you hearing me and smiling over the details that make up my life now. I never tell you how defeated I feel at moments or how hard I work to hide it from everyone for fear they will see it as a reason to stop believing you are coming home to us.

And I couldn't tell you about the lump I found in my breast and how difficult it was going through all the tests without you here to lean on. The lump was benign—the process reaching that diagnosis utterly terrifying. I couldn't stop thinking about what would happen to Shelly and Jason if something happened to me.

We need you to come home.

I'm worn down with missing you.

I'm going to read this tomorrow and will probably tear it up or burn it in the fireplace. I don't want you to get the idea I ever doubted what I was doing to free you or thought the work a burden. I would gladly spend the rest of my life at it, even if, in the end, we only had one day together.

You are my life, Evan.

I will love you forever.

* * * * *

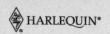

HARLEQUIN® *Romance*®

presents a brand-new trilogy by

PATRICIA THAYER

Rocky Mountain
B R I D E S

Three sisters come home to wed.

In April don't miss
Raising the Rancher's Family,

followed by

The Sheriff's Pregnant Wife,

on sale May 2007,

and

A Mother for the Tycoon's Child,

on sale June 2007.

From *New York Times* bestselling author
SHERRYL WOODS
The Sweet Magnolias

February 2007   **March 2007**   **April 2007**

SAVE
$1.00 off the purchase price of any book in *The Sweet Magnolias* trilogy.

Offer valid from February 1, 2007 to April 30, 2007. Redeemable at participating retail outlets. Limit one coupon per purchase.

52607602

5 65373 00076 2 (8100) 0 11383

MSWSMT07

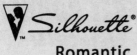

Silhouette® Romantic SUSPENSE

Excitement, danger and passion guaranteed!

USA TODAY bestselling author
Marie Ferrarella
is back with the second installment
in her popular miniseries,
*The Doctors Pulaski: Medicine
just got more interesting...*
DIAGNOSIS: DANGER is on sale
April 2007 from Silhouette®
Romantic Suspense (formerly
Silhouette Intimate Moments).

*Look for it wherever
you buy books!*

REQUEST YOUR FREE BOOKS!
2 FREE NOVELS PLUS 2 FREE GIFTS!

SPECIAL EDITION®
Life, Love and Family!

YES! Please send me 2 FREE Silhouette Special Edition® novels and my 2 FREE gifts. After receiving them, if I don't wish to receive any more books, I can return the shipping statement marked "cancel." If I don't cancel, I will receive 6 brand-new novels every month and be billed just $4.24 per book in the U.S., or $4.99 per book in Canada, plus 25¢ shipping and handling per book and applicable taxes, if any*. That's a savings of at least 15% off the cover price! I understand that accepting the 2 free books and gifts places me under no obligation to buy anything. I can always return a shipment and cancel at any time. Even if I never buy another book from Silhouette, the two free books and gifts are mine to keep forever.

235 SDN EEYU 335 SDN EEY6

Name	(PLEASE PRINT)
Address	Apt.
City	State/Prov.	Zip/Postal Code

Signature (if under 18, a parent or guardian must sign)

Mail to the Silhouette Reader Service™:
IN U.S.A.: P.O. Box 1867, Buffalo, NY 14240-1867
IN CANADA: P.O. Box 609, Fort Erie, Ontario L2A 5X3

Not valid to current Silhouette Special Edition subscribers.

Want to try two free books from another line?
Call 1-800-873-8635 or visit www.morefreebooks.com.

* Terms and prices subject to change without notice. NY residents add applicable sales tax. Canadian residents will be charged applicable provincial taxes and GST. This offer is limited to one order per household. All orders subject to approval. Credit or debit balances in a customer's account(s) may be offset by any other outstanding balance owed by or to the customer. Please allow 4 to 6 weeks for delivery.

Your Privacy: Silhouette is committed to protecting your privacy. Our Privacy Policy is available online at www.eHarlequin.com or upon request from the Reader Service. From time to time we make our lists of customers available to reputable firms who may have a product or service of interest to you. If you would prefer we not share your name and address, please check here. ☐

SSE07

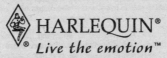

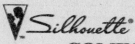

COMING NEXT MONTH

SSECNM0307